A POTION FOR YOUR THOUGHTS

AN (UN)LUCKY VALLEY NOVELLA

BOOK THREE

MICHELLE M. PILLOW

MICHELLEPILLOW.COM

ABOUT A POTION FOR YOUR THOUGHTS

From NY Times & USA TODAY Bestselling Author, Michelle M. Pillow, a Cozy Mystery Paranormal Romantic Comedy.

Where the magic of love meets the power of the paranormal, the spell is unbreakable.

Jesse Goode has spent the last two years avoiding going to Lucky Valley, Colorado, to claim an inheritance she doesn't want. But when supernatural dangers threaten the only thing she cares about, she has no choice.

(Un)Lucky Valley Novella
A Paranormal Cozy Mystery Romance

(UN)LUCKY VALLEY SERIES

Better Haunts and Garden Gnomes
Any Witch Way But Goode
A Potion for Your Thoughts

Happily Everlasting - Prequel Books
Featuring Aunt Polly
Fooled Around and Spelled in Love
Curses and Cupcakes

AUTHOR UPDATES

To stay informed about when a new book in the series installments is released, sign up for updates:

http://michellepillow.com/author-updates/

To a wonderfully talented group of authors in the witch romance anthology where this was originally published: Mandy M. Roth, Deanna Chase, T.M. Cromer, V Vaughn, Yasmine Galenorn, Amy Boyles, Renee George, Sarah Hegger, Stephanie Berchiolly, Jennifer Blackstream, Christina Garner.

It's been a pleasure working with you all!

CHAPTER ONE

SPOKANE, Washington

"Jessamine Rosemary Goode?"

Jesse glanced at the man's outstretched hand and kept walking. Her boss didn't put up with tardiness, and she wasn't about to lose her job because a bill collector decided to track her down outside her apartment building. It had already been a rough morning. Her kitchen faucet had literally shot off its base, and her kitchen was now decorated with wet towels.

"Excuse me, are you—?"

"Nope," Jesse answered, walking faster and not making eye contact. She gripped her rolled apron in her hand.

The man stood next to a blue sedan. She'd detected the rental sticker in the car's window.

Seeing the bus, she jogged toward it and hopped on. Only when she found a seat did she turn her attention back down the sidewalk. She couldn't make out much of his face, but the man watched the bus.

Mrs. Candy, as the kids in the building called her because of the jar of hard candy, she kept by her door for them, came down the sidewalk with her walker. A plastic grocery bag hung from one of the handles. The man instantly turned to offer his help.

Jesse leaned her head to watch the show, but the moving bus forced the scene out of view. Too bad. Mrs. Candy would probably try to throw her walker at him for treating her like she was helpless.

"Tough old bird," Jesse muttered with a laugh. She'd been on the other end of that woman's sharp tongue more than once.

The bus only went a few blocks before stopping to let her off. Normally she wouldn't waste a ride, but she didn't need Mr. Bill Collector following her.

A restaurant called The Bulb Tavern might not sound like a strict place to work, but the owner had no problem firing people for even the slightest infraction. Usually, she would have told Robert to shove the job where the sun didn't shine, but the truth was she made more in tips on the weekends than she would from working a hundred hours a week anywhere else.

Plus, being a waitress made her feel normal.

Twinkly fairy lights surrounded the wooden bar and draped across the ceiling. During the day, they were white, but as the evening wore on, they'd start slowly fading through a spectrum of colors. A waitress once commented that she felt like they worked under a Christmas tree, and Jesse could not get the description out of her head.

Jesse tied the half-apron around her waist as she walked through the empty restaurant. They didn't open for another ten minutes. Seeing the blue rental car pulling up outside, she frowned.

"Did you clock in?" Robert asked, coming from his back office. He tapped his naked wrist to indicate a watch.

"On my way," Jesse answered, not breaking stride. She would hate to forget and miss out on that two dollars and ten cents an hour come payday. Thank goodness for tippers.

"We need side salads," he said.

"Always do," Jesse mumbled under her breath.

Out of habit, she started to pull her name tag out of her apron and then stopped. She again looked outside to see the man getting out of the car. He stared up at the restaurant sign above the door.

Seeing the hostess in the wait station, she said, "Paula, do me a favor. If some guy comes in asking for me, tell him you have no clue who he's talking about."

Paula wore too bright a shade of red lipstick and looked like she was perpetually bored. "Stalker?"

"I wish," Jesse answered. She went to a box that had discarded name tags from past employees and dug around inside. "Bill collector."

"Hate them," Paula said. She stopped on her way to the hostess stand and turned around to give Jesse a strange look. "I hate rom-coms too. It gives me a false sense of hope that someday I'll fall in love when I know I'm unlovable."

"Um, okay?" Jesse frowned at the impromptu confession. Those kinds of weird comments have been happening quite a bit lately. Last night, her neighbor had cornered her in the hallway to discuss his mother's hysterectomy. Jesse had been trapped for an hour holding a bag of groceries.

She pulled out a couple of tags, discarding the names of Joe and Marge before settling on the third. She pinned it to her shirt. "Hello, my name is Rita."

Nina heard her as she went to punch in at the time clock and laughed. "I want to play. Hand me one of those."

Jesse tossed Marge at her.

Catching it, Nina laughed harder. "Marge, here to service you."

"Dirty." Jesse clocked in.

"Well, Marge is a bad girl." Nina grinned briefly, and then her expression fell. "My grandma used to tell me I was bad all the time. I guess I grew up to prove her right."

Jesse just stared at her. Nina shrugged and started smiling again.

"We need salads," Jesse pushed the task onto Nina as she went to check the dining room.

"Always do," Nina answered.

Robert came toward them as she was trying to peek out. "Jess, Paula gave you a single. You're on section two tonight."

Jesse nodded, retreating to make a glass of ice water before Robert could tell her about some childhood trauma.

Approaching her section, Jesse nearly tripped as dark eyes met hers. Mr. Bill Collector was cuter than she thought he'd be. Before when they'd crossed paths, she had willfully not looked in his direction for too long.

Cute or not, he wasn't her usual type. The man's hair was neatly cut in a short style popular with lawyers and bankers, and he wore slacks with a button-down. Jesse tended to go for the rocker, cheat-with-your-friends, never-lose-your-heart, loser types like Vance. She used to think she wanted a man who made her laugh, played by his own rules, and didn't need to be told what to do every second of the day. It turns out that combination equaled a charming womanizer who spent more time lying than breathing.

The problem was that no one could lie to her, at least not for any actual length of time. For some reason, if she listened long enough, they confessed every sin they ever committed.

Maybe she needed someone like Bill Collector here—someone good with numbers who filed their taxes on time and who probably did things like play Dungeons and Dragons and was only late because the side quest or whatever went into overtime. It might be interesting, and she was sure she could persuade him to delete her billing account.

Jesse pushed the thought out of her head. She didn't have time for love, a boyfriend, or whomever she imagined sat at her table.

"Can I get you something else to drink?" Jesse put the water down in front of him and pulled a pen and pad from her apron.

"Hey, I saw you outside," he answered. "You're Jessamine, right?"

Nice try, buddy.

Sure, this was a coincidence. Like he didn't follow her to work.

"Rita." She tapped the tag with the end of her pen. "Anything to drink, sir?"

"Coffee," he answered. "Is there a reason—?"

"Coffee. Be right back." Jesse went to fetch the coffee. Hopefully, this would be the end of his search. Her rudeness would probably be the end of her tip.

A loud clicking noise came from the server station, sounding like the stamping of the time clock on repeat.

"Hey, Jess, were you able to clock in?" Cameron from the kitchen held his timecard, unable to force it into the slot. "I need the hours. My roommate wants to buy tickets to—"

"That's weird. Go get Robert," she said, cutting off his story.

Jesse didn't stop to help him as she grabbed the coffee and returned to the collection agent. When she went to set the drink down on the table, a picture caught her attention. Her family photo stared up at her from the dark finish. The man pointed at the faces. "That's your sister Lily. Your brother, Dante, and that," he tapped several times on her younger face, "is Jessamine Goode."

Jesse frowned and briefly considered making a joke about some long-lost twin, but the words wouldn't come. She stared at the photo for a little too long. She hadn't expected to see her siblings —or feel the wave of longing that washed over her. She missed them deeply. It had been a year since they had been together when Lily and Dante had visited her in Spokane.

Two years ago, her siblings had decided to go to Lucky Valley, Colorado, to accept an inheritance from their estranged mother. Jesse couldn't bring herself to visit them there. The few times she had gotten into the car to drive, her hands had shaken so badly she couldn't start the engine, and she'd felt nauseous. She wanted nothing to do with their mother. The woman had been dead for about seven years, and the thought of going to Colorado to deal with the estate caused a knot of anger in her stomach.

"I prefer Rita," Jesse drawled, giving up the charade.

"I prefer Jessamine like the flower." He

smiled. Was he flirting with her? "It's very pretty."

"Dude, stop. No one calls me that. It's Jesse." She glanced around to check if her boss was watching before adding, "Besides, you say flower. I say poisonous toxin. Pretty to look at but get too close, and the alkaloids can kill you. If you're not here about the payment for a car I don't have anymore because someone set it on fire three months ago, why are you hassling me?"

"Someone set your car on fire?" He looked surprised. "That sounds unfortunate."

"What can I say? I live a fascinating life." Jesse shrugged. Unfortunate was a mild way of putting it. Her luck hadn't been the greatest lately. "By your reaction, I take it you're not a bill collector?"

"No. I'm Malachi Rhodes from MacIver Law in Lucky Valley, Colorado." He held out his hand. "We've spoken on the phone a few times, and then you changed your phone number."

Jesse didn't touch him as she arched a brow. His voice sounded familiar, but he didn't look anything like what she'd imagined. "*You're* Malachi, like from the cornfield horror movie Malachi?"

"I still don't get that joke." He lowered his hand to the table. "Friends call me Mal."

"No offense, but you don't look anything like your phone voice." It had been over six months since she'd changed her number to stop calls from an ex-one-date who couldn't handle rejection. Maybe if she'd realized whom she was talking to, she wouldn't have been so hasty.

He kept smiling. The playful expression reached his eyes. "What does my voice look like?"

"Some gray-haired lawyer with one of those business-in-the-front, party-in-the-back mullets," she answered candidly.

"So, you're into gray hair?" He leaned over and pointed toward his temple. "I've been working on a few."

"Who says I'm into you?" Jesse chuckled. "That's presumptuous."

"Ouch." He put his hand over his heart. "You look exactly like your voice."

"You had a picture." Jesse pointed at the family photo. "So, Mal Rhodes from MacIver Law? What brings you to Spokane?"

She had a feeling she knew the answer. It would be the same reason why he'd called.

"I'm here on behalf of the estate of Marigold Crawford Goode." He reached next to him to flip open a leather case. "She left—"

"Nope," Jesse shook her head.

"Excuse me?" He stopped mid-action.

"Not interested."

"But—"

"I thought my not showing up to the reading of the will or answering your many, many, *many* letters would have been hint enough. Or the fact I repeatedly told you as much on the phone."

"I don't remember that part of the phone calls." His smile was a little too charming. "I remember you talking about red nail polish on your toes."

"Mr. Rhodes, please hear me. I don't want anything from Marigold Crawford Goode. When I was little, I did. I wanted a mother who gave a damn. Instead, I got a woman who left my siblings and me to starve to death in a car. I don't care if she had her reasons. We all have our reasons for doing things. Her actions—"

A short whistle sounded, and she glanced toward the bar. Robert stared at her and nodded his head to speed things along.

"Now, if that's all, I have to get back to work. I've been told the salads won't make themselves." She made a show of holding her notepad and pen. "You want a sandwich or something? We need to prep for the rush. There's a bookseller's convention down the street, and they all come in between their scheduled meetings."

"We can't close the matter until you officially refuse—" he tried to explain.

"I officially refuse," she interrupted.

"What?"

"Everything. I don't want anything from her. Let Lily and Dante and that other one, Mara, keep it all."

Apparently, Marigold had another baby after she'd abandoned the first three. Jesse had only talked to Mara a handful of times on video chats. It wasn't enough to build any meaningful relationship.

Mara had been born in a barn—an actual freaking barn because her dad was a demon-ghost or whatever. Jesse took it to mean he'd been a real bastard. The conversations since her siblings moved had become a little strange. Jesse wanted nothing to do with witchcraft or family magic. Sure, she could admit it was fun to believe in things like hauntings and ghosts, but she didn't have proof that any of it was real.

Talking to her siblings, it all sounded insane. Jesse wanted normal.

"Actually, yeah," Jesse decided, "give it to Mara. It sounds like she might need it to pay for therapy."

"You do know, don't you? You know who you are. You know what is involved."

Jesse frowned. What was this man's problem? Why could no one at the MacIver office take no for an answer?

"Do I know that there's money involved?" Jesse questioned. "That I'm an heiress, and if I just say yes, all my money problems will disappear? Like that's going to make up for a lifetime of—"

Another short whistle sounded. Her boss really was a jerk.

Jesse swiped the family photo and shoved it in her apron beside her phone. She didn't owe him or anyone an explanation. This was her life, and she would live it her way.

"Enjoy your coffee, Mr. Rhodes." She strode away from the table.

Robert gave her a stern look, and she held her hand up to calm him down.

"I'm not paying you to date," Robert said as she strode past.

"Going to make salads now," she lied and hurried into the server station.

CHAPTER TWO

MAL WATCHED Jesse move across the restaurant from inside his car. She really was in denial about her supernatural gifts, or she hid them well. Everyone knew that the Crawfords and Goodes were both family lines of powerful witches, two of the oldest known in history, and Jesse was a product of both. That alliance terrified people. Since the moment Marigold Crawford and Joseph Goode fell in love, fear ran rampant in Lucky Valley. The birth of their children only made it worse.

Then Marigold Crawford Goode started showing signs of insanity, and the rumors exploded from there. So did the town's run of terrible luck. If even a third of the rumors about the woman were true, he couldn't say he blamed

Jesse for not wanting anything to do with her eccentric mother.

Still, her siblings were in Lucky Valley. Everyone at the firm thought she'd eventually show up in town, at least for a visit. It never happened.

Even though he preferred logic to folklore and superstition, he had to admit that a part of him was frightened by Jesse. Since Lily and Dante moved to town two years ago, everyone had been tense, as if waiting for some giant magical flareup to take them all out.

Mal had drawn the short straw and had been sent to Washington state to fetch her. Well, in truth, he'd rigged the short straw so that they'd send him. Those few phone calls had played themselves over in his mind, and he's stared at her legal file more often than he should have. More to the point, he stared at the picture in her legal file.

Practicing law in Lucky Valley wasn't like in other places. The town was home to supernatural creatures, and they preferred to keep that fact a secret. When a vampire had a problem with a neighbor cutting down a row of shade trees on the property line, it wasn't just an annoyance. It could be life or death for the vampire. That meant attempted murder charges.

Or when the sweet-tempered neighborhood grandma wolfed out with the full moon and ended up arrested on vandalism charges, someone needed to argue that it was temporary moon insanity.

Or when the Hellmouth broke open because teenagers were messing with books they shouldn't have, it could be argued that the devil made them do it.

These were not things that would hold up in most courts.

All of those cases were nothing compared to dealing with the Goodes.

Hardly anyone in town trusted the family, which really was the nicest way Mal could think to say it. The truth was that the residents of Lucky Valley blamed the Crawfords and the Goodes for the run of bad luck that had plagued the town since the original Lucky Valley had sprung up as an old mining camp.

Souffle fell? Goodes were to blame.

Goblins hoarding in the park? Yep, the Goodes had something to do with that.

Vampires getting too bitey with the tourists? Surely the Goodes' magic caused the abnormal behavior.

House fire? Frozen pipes? Car crash? Stuck in traffic? Goodes. Goodes. Goodes. Goodes.

Even when their house had stood empty, and none of them could be found for miles, the family was still blamed.

It wasn't just that they were powerful. They were rich too. The Goode Family Trust also owned an enormous amount of property, which included the defunct mines and the nearby ghost town of Old Lucky Valley, which the locals had nicknamed Unlucky Valley.

Mal felt like a creeper, but he couldn't stop staring. Jesse's pictures didn't do her justice. There was an energy about her when she moved and talked. It radiated like a swarm of angry bees stuck in a sack.

And oh, how he wanted to be stung.

His family had warned him to remain disciplined when it came to attraction. The little bit of elf heritage could cause him to become too easily attached.

Jesse's work uniform consisted of jeans, sneakers, and a logoed shirt. Her wavy brown hair was pulled into a chaotic mess on the top of her head. She didn't wear much makeup, not that she needed to. Her hazel eyes looked to be a stunning mixture of green and brown.

A loud knock sounded on his window, causing him to jump in his seat.

Thick, pink plastic glasses with tiny fake

gemstones framed the woman's eyes. Bright red hair that could not have grown naturally from anything radiated around her face in a frizz of curls. She grinned and motioned for him to crank down the window.

Mal hit the power button and slid it down. "Hey, Polly, what are you doing here?"

"I'm always where I'm supposed to be. But I could ask you the same thing." Polly Crawford circled her finger as she pointed it at him. The gesture made him nervous. He couldn't tell if she was being playful or trying to cast a spell on him. The witch had to be at least in her fifties, maybe older, but she had the playful energy of a teenager.

"Law firm business. We're trying to close out the Goode will," he said. "Are you visiting your niece?"

"Sunspots," she said, stepping back as if expecting him to get out of the car. A large pink purse hung from her arm. Traffic zoomed around her, honking. She smiled and waved at the taillights.

"Polly, wait, damn it." Mal hurried out of the car and grabbed her arm to pull her to safety. She was known as an eccentric about town and didn't appear to notice that people were scared of her. He released her arm when they stood on the sidewalk by The Bulb Tavern. "What do you mean, sunspots?"

"I looked into the sun, and my eyes got all spotty in the shape of Jesse's face. You know how it is, sugar bee," she quipped, swaying back and forth. "Bippity, bap, and thump-bump-bump."

"Polly?" He tried to get her attention to focus, but she was too busy dancing in a circle.

She wore what looked to be a square-dancing costume with a giant petticoat skirt. The pink gingham was a softer shade than her glasses and purse. Pink cowboy boots sparkled with tiny gems. Suddenly she stopped as a small smile crossed her features, and she elbowed him in the ribs. "You like angry bees, don't you? *Buzz, buzz!*"

Mal instantly glanced inside at Jesse, who was speaking to her boss near the bar. There was no way Polly could have known his thoughts about a sack of bees. Could she?

Mal wondered if Polly had ever talked to someone about her strange tendencies and verbal flights of fancy. Or maybe it was a case of breathing in too many of the family potion fumes over the years. Perhaps insanity was a side effect of generations of magic. Marigold had suffered under its strain.

He again looked at Jesse. Did she suffer as well?

"That looks dangerous. Here, hold Herman for me." Polly thrust the purse at him. "I'm going in."

"Dangerous?" Mal caught the purse.

Jesse looked fine to him. Her boss was laughing as he said something to her.

"Wait, Herman?" Mal asked. As Polly strode toward the door, he couldn't resist looking inside the bag. A live lobster twitched as if to look up at him from a cotton bed of fabric. The crustacean wore a blue Hawaiian shirt with a tiny lei around his neck. "Hi."

Herman snapped his pinchers in response. Mal quickly closed the bag.

A couple walked by. The man took notice of the purse and frowned in disapproval before giving a snort.

"Nothing to see here," Mal said loudly after him. "Just a man with a fabulous handbag."

The couple walked faster. Mal gave a small laugh.

When he turned his attention back to the window, he saw a flurry of movement. Polly threw a glass toward Jesse's boss while Jesse tried to pull her back.

"Oh, crap!" Mal rushed through the door. He wasn't sure where he could be of help, so he stopped to watch what was happening to gauge the situation. Two powerful witches probably didn't need a man to protect them.

"You will not speak to my niece like that. Apologize at once," Polly demanded. The customers watched the display in shock. "Don't make me glue your mouth shut until you learn some manners, young man! There will be no dibble-dabbling of the staff."

"Jesse, get her out of here, or I'm calling the cops…" her boss demanded.

"Oh, yeah, do that. They have the pretty lights," Polly spoke over him with a laugh.

"…and clean up this mess," he finished.

"No cookies for Mr. Robert," Polly stated. "Not until you apologize."

"Get that crazy bitc—" Robert began.

"Hey!" Mal stated in warning at the same time that Jesse demanded, "Don't."

Jesse held up her hand toward Robert. "Do not finish…"

"You can have cookies, though," Polly told a woman. "You're a good sort."

"That's it. I'm done. Get out," Robert ordered. "You're fired. Take her with you. I have applications a mile high from girls wanting this job. I don't need the headache."

"You have warts on your feet," Polly announced.

Robert launched a towel at them. "Get out!"

"Good one, Polly," Jesse drawled wryly before ushering the older woman toward the door. "Let's get out of here."

Jesse glanced at Mal in confusion as he held open the door for them. "You're still here."

"Our conversation—" he started to explain.

"I apologize for my harsh language," Polly said once she was outside. "That one riled me more than a sock full of nickels in a dime candy store."

"I don't know what half the things you say mean," Jesse muttered.

"Candy should be a nickel," Polly stated as if that were a known fact everyone could agree on.

Mal tried to hand Polly her lobster purse.

Polly waved her hand at the door. "Good riddance, pumpkin doodle. Enough with this life waystation."

"Polly, what are you doing here?" Jesse asked.

"I came for you," Polly said. "Get in the car. I'm driving."

"Where?" Jesse asked.

"Road trip to your destiny," Polly answered. "It's time."

"I can't go on a road trip. I have to work," Jesse denied.

"No. You don't have a job," Poly countered.

"I mean, I need to work. I have to find a new job." Jesse started walking toward her apartment.

"Is that all? I'll hire you," Polly said.

"To do what?" Jesse sighed in noticeable exasperation.

"I have a maid service called *Polly's Perfectly Magical Mystical Maids, Mops, and Lollipops*. You can pass out the lollipops. I'll even let you eat a few and they won't cost you a nickel."

"Um, no." Jesse didn't even pretend to consider it.

Polly waved at Mal to follow as she chased after Jesse. "What about a tour guide for *Polly's Mostly Magical Fantastical Foray into Mysterious Worlds of Wonder*? You can help me get Lily to agree to let me open it. We can drop tourists down the mine shafts in Old Lucky Valley."

"That's not a good idea—" Mal tried to interrupt.

"No." Jesse walked faster.

"I'd offer a place in my magic shop, *Polly's Perfectly Magical Mystical Wondrous World of Wonders*, but it's in Maine in the back of a coffee shop. I think you'd be better off in Colorado with your siblings while the magic settles."

"How many businesses do you have?" Mal asked.

Polly didn't answer him.

Jesse suddenly stopped and looked toward the ground for several deep breaths.

Polly reached to open her purse while Mal still held it. She patted the lobster on the head before digging next to him to produce a small potion vial. She shook it in her hand.

"I'm not going to move to Colorado," Jesse said at last. She turned to stare at them. "I need you both to hear me. I don't want the inheritance. Mail me the paperwork, and I promise I'll sign it."

"It's more than paperwork. There's a safe deposit box you must be present to open," Mal said.

"I'll sign a waiver," Jesse countered. "You do it. I don't want—"

"Oh, pumpkin doodle, did I forget to mention that Lily hasn't been well?" Polly opened the potion bottle. "It's time for you to come home. Fate doesn't tap dance. It salsas."

Jesse's expression fell into one of concern. "What do you mean? Is she sick?"

"She's sad," Polly said. "She misses you."

Jesse grimaced. "Stop trying to manipulate me."

"Here, put this on," Polly jerked her hand to toss the potion bottle's contents on Jesse.

Jesse swatted to stop the onslaught. Suddenly her hands fell to her side, and she blinked slowly.

"Hey, what is that?" Mal demanded. "What did you do?"

"Small cosmic realignment," Polly answered. "Help her into the car."

"We're not kidnapping your niece." Mal refused to help her.

"You're here because that box is causing trouble, right?" Polly insisted with a tilt of her head. "Things waking up that shouldn't be?"

Mal frowned. No one else was supposed to know about that.

Jesse blinked as if confused and numb.

Polly pointed a thumb at her niece. "You need to get this one to that one, right?"

"There are some concerns, but I'm not forcing—" Mal thrust the purse at Polly. "I'll take her home and stay with her until this potion wears off. I'll try talking to her again."

"Be a man of action," Polly said. "Like my Petey."

"I don't know Petey," Mal countered.

"He's a man of action," Polly insisted. Her purse began to thump as Herman thrashed around inside. She ignored it. "Do you know what we're dealing with, young man? You've heard of Pandora's box, right?"

"Yes," Mal stated.

Polly instantly opened the bag and soothed, "Oh, hey, easy little love. We'll have your Hawaiian party."

"Polly?" Mal wanted to shake the older woman and make her concentrate.

Polly reached into her bag, and suddenly, colorful lights began emanating from within. "Have fun."

"I know you." A blonde stopped beside Jesse.

Polly closed her bag. The muffled sounds of a ukulele came from within.

Jesse ignored her aunt. She merely blinked and looked at the blonde woman talking to her.

"Your hair is fantastic," the woman continued, patting her short shag. "I've always wanted thicker hair. Mine is so fine, and my scalp is sensitive. My mother would brush it like she was pulling weeds. Hurt like hell. She was a nasty piece of work. Used to—"

"That's fine, deary." Polly lifted her hand to guide the woman along. "Keep it moving. Tell it to that nice man who delivers mail to your office. He'd love to hear all about it."

"Harry?" the blonde asked in confusion as she stumbled away.

Mal brushed off the woman's interruption.

"Polly, please tell me your family doesn't have Pandora's actual box."

"Of course not." Polly laughed.

Mal started to relax. The witch inched closer to him.

"This thing makes Pandora's look like a plastic jewelry box with a broken latch," Polly whispered, tapping her finger against her lips to indicate a secret.

Mal stared at Jesse. All thoughts of attraction and protection had to be set aside. "It's been…leaking."

"I told you. Fate doesn't tap dance. Right now, it's tired of being a wallflower." Polly turned to Jesse. "Jesse, do you want to see Lily and Dante?"

"Yes, please." Jesse nodded. "Can you take me to them?"

"Sure thing." Polly looked at her expectantly. "Do you have a cat, or dog, or python, or fish that needs to be taken care of?"

Jesse shook her head. "Not even a plant."

"No familiar yet, either." Polly shook her head. "Maybe you're more Crawford than Goode. Not all Crawfords have pets."

"I don't have a pet. I can barely take care of myself," Jesse mumbled.

"See there, Mr. Frownie Face, no kidnapping.

Hand me the keys." Polly held out her hand expectantly.

"No." Mal glanced around. Robert stood in the restaurant's window, arms crossed, glaring at them. The hard man's gaze made Mal uncomfortable. "I'm driving."

Mal guided Jesse gently by the arm toward the passenger seat.

"You're a lot cuter voice in person," she told him.

"Uh, thanks." Mal wasn't sure if he was doing the right thing.

Well, yes, for the town of Lucky Valley with a leaking Pandora-like box, he was doing the right thing. For Jesse? He wasn't sure.

"Bipity bap." Polly gave a little dance along the curb before hopping onto the busy street.

"I'll call the office and see if we can get flights. It's a sixteen-hour drive before you add on stops." Mal didn't think he could spend a day driving with Polly.

"Trust me, driving is faster. I can get us there in three hours, maybe two," Polly said. "You just steer. Herman and I will navigate."

CHAPTER THREE

Jesse heard voices, but they sounded muffled as if coming from another room. Her eyes focused on the road ahead, and she barely noted the passing countryside or trees. They all seemed to blur together. Within those blurs, creatures appeared to emerge, strange beings with gnarled bodies and terrifying faces.

Mal drove the car, gripping the steering wheel like he battled with the vehicle for dominance. Sweat lined his brow. His were some of the muttered words she couldn't quite make out.

"I like your hands," she told him, not considering she shouldn't say what was on her mind. "They're worker's hands. Not all soft like I imagined a lawyer with a mullet ponytail might be."

He glanced at her with a worried expression. "Thanks. I like your hands too."

Jesse heard a splash and turned to find a lobster in a small tray next to her aunt in the backseat. A garden gnome holding a sign that read, "Listen to me," was seat belted in.

She had only discovered she had an Aunt Polly around the same time she'd learned there was a will. She had been one of Marigold's friends when they were young, as well as a distant cousin.

"I see things," Jesse said to Polly, trying to explain.

"I know, pumpkin doodle," Polly answered, placing a tiny hat on the lobster's head. "They mean you no harm. We're just speeding up your latent magic. Giving it a good goose on the backside."

A knock sounded on her window, and she turned to find a man staring at her. She frowned, confused. When had the car stopped?

She turned to ask Mal, but he was gone. Her movements felt wooden, like after a night of one too many glasses of wine.

The knock sounded again. The man smiled expectantly. Jesse hit the button to roll down the window. They were by gas pumps. She didn't remember turning off the interstate.

The man instantly launched into a rush of words. "My son told me last night that he doesn't want to attend college. We have been saving since he was a baby, working hellish hours so he doesn't have to get a loan. He's only thirteen. I think he's just confused, but my wife wants to go on a cruise now—"

Jesse didn't answer as she reversed the direction of the window to block him out. He kept talking, the jumbled words coming faster as his lips followed the closing gap of the window.

A young woman appeared next to the man, holding a cellphone. She tried to weave around the college dad as if to show Jesse its screen. A minivan pulled up to the pumps, and a couple exited the vehicle. The woman reached for the gas pump as her husband started to head inside the station. Suddenly, they both turned and stopped what they were doing as they came toward the line forming outside of Jesse's window.

"Do I let her spend the money on a cruise?" College Dad persisted, knocking on the glass.

"What do you think of this text?" Phone Girl yelled as she waved her cellphone. "Do you believe what he's saying? Is he with Charlotte?"

"My son is carsick," the husband from the minivan stated. "My wife wants to stop for the night, but I want to push on another five hours."

"He wants to get home to his mistress," Minivan Wife shouted.

"I don't have a mistress," Minivan Husband argued. "Tell her I don't have a mistress."

"Um, Polly?" Jesse asked, worried. The glass doors of the gas station opened, and more people came outside to head toward her. She gripped the edge of her seat, her fingers kneading the material in worry.

For some reason, she got the impression that, yes, the boyfriend was with Charlotte.

And thirteen was too young to make any life plan. If they kept the money, the kid would be a dermatologist. If they didn't, he'd own a small business. Both were fine paths, but who the hell knew what they wanted to be at thirteen?

And Minivan Husband didn't have a mistress, but the wife did.

"Back off!" Mal yelled, running past the gathering crowd. He carried two bags of groceries.

He slid into the driver's seat and tossed the bags on Jesse's lap. The engine revved as he quickly drove them out of there. A few of the people jogged after the car.

"Oh, good, snacks!" Polly exclaimed. "Pass those back. Herman needs his travel chips."

Jesse handed the bags to the backseat.

"Lobsters like chips?" Mal asked Jesse.

"I…" She gave a small shrug and turned to look back at the station.

"What was that all about?" he asked.

"They just wanted to talk to me." She turned her attention forward. "They thought I could give them advice or something. It's weird. It's like I have some kind of cosmic sign on my head that says, tell me your trauma, ask me your fate."

"Penny for your thoughts," Polly laughed.

"The potion?" Mal glanced into the rearview mirror as if to stare at Polly.

"Potion for your thoughts," Polly amended. "I like that."

"What potion?" Jesse felt as if her mind was clearing. "Why am I…? Where are we…? Wait. Polly, what did you do?"

"Cosmic realignment. Like rotating car tires," Polly responded. "You are two years, five days, and a handful of hours past your due date. You're throwing off the magical balance."

"Why does no one from Lucky Valley ever make sense?" Jesse stared at Mal, waiting for an answer. Out of the two others in the car, he seemed to be the candidate for the sanest.

Instead, he changed the subject. "You look like you're feeling better. What was that about at the restaurant with your boss?"

"I don't even know. One minute I'm waiting on my table's Rum Strawberry Surprise, and the next, he's confessing his attraction and talking about giving me a raise if I give *him* a raise." Jesse grimaced. She looked down and realized she still wore her half-apron. Feeling the pockets, she found her wallet and phone inside. She leaned forward in her seat to untie it. "I could have handled it, but Polly took offense on my behalf and called him out publicly. It sucks, too. I was good at that job, and the tips were decent."

"He's lucky I didn't call his mama for a grounding," Polly said.

Jesse had another sudden impression of Robert fearing his mother's disapproval. It was something she couldn't have known.

The car jerked and began making a banging noise.

"What the…?" Mal started to slow.

"Here, Jesse, hold this," Polly said.

Jesse automatically reached back. Cool liquid covered her fingers. She felt the world begin to blur again.

"Keep driving," Polly said. "That should hold us the rest of the trip."

"Jesse?" Mal asked.

She blinked, unable to form words, as she looked at him.

"Damn it, Polly, what did you do?" Mal demanded.

"Just a potion for her thoughts. We need her powers charged and understood before we get there. Silly thing. She's still trying to deny her magic." Polly leaned over with a bag of potato chips. "Hungry?"

Mal frowned but snatched the bag. "Hand me those pretzel pieces too."

"That a boy!" Polly exclaimed.

Jesse turned her attention back to the creatures forming outside the windows within the blurry landscape.

CHAPTER FOUR

Garden Gnome Bed and Breakfast, Lucky Valley, Colorado

Jesse had seen the Victorian home that Lily had converted into a bed-and-breakfast while on video calls with her siblings. The lone house stood like a solitary pink blight on the mountainous countryside. She hadn't been a fan of the girly color when she saw it on screen, but now it blended with the reds and purples of the sun setting in the background.

The Victorian seemed to be at a natural crossroads where the forest met mountains met a valley. Trees arched around the back of the house. Mountains filled the view to the left of the house with a valley rolling to the right.

Chubby faces stared at them from all around

the lawn, like a garden gnome welcome commit-tee. Their pointy hats and long beards were cute, if not a little kitschy. None of this made her think of Dante and Lily.

"There doesn't seem to be any guests," Jesse said, eyeing the one car in the driveway. When they came to a stop, she didn't get out. She had a difficult time imagining her siblings being happy here.

"Nolan put up cabins. They rent those out. I don't think many guests stay in the house anymore," Mal said. After a long moment of her staring, he lightly touched her arm. "Are you all right being here?"

The contact took her by surprise, pulling her out of her stupor. She took a deep breath and nodded. His eyes held hers, and his hand didn't leave her. There was a calmness to his presence. How had she not noticed that before? "I can't believe I'm here. I told myself I'd never step foot in this place."

"I can give you a ride to town for the night if you'd rather," he offered.

"Don't be ridiculous," Polly stated, popping up between the seats to break their eye contact. His hand dropped from her arm. "She belongs here."

Jesse leaned forward to reconnect her gaze

with Mal's. "Lily said they were in the city limits. I thought this was in town. It looks like the middle of nowhere."

"Technically, this is in city limits," he said, clearing his throat. "Before we were able to locate Marigold's heirs, there was a rezoning that took place. It was supposed to make it easier for the town to take over the property as abandoned."

"Steal it," Polly inserted. "Like little goblins in the night after porridge."

"Polly, can we have a moment?" Jesse asked.

"I'll tell Lily you're here." Polly gathered Herman and got out of the car. "The stars told me you wouldn't kiss her yet, so I'm not missing anything."

Jesse grimaced as Polly shut the door. "I'm sorry about her. She's…"

"Interesting," Mal finished.

Jesse nodded. Polly's words hung between them as if predicting what may come. It only made the moment awkward.

"Did you want to talk to me about something now that she's gone?" he asked.

"I think I have magical powers," Jesse said.

He simply nodded. She had expected a bigger reaction.

"Like magic."

"I know. You come from a family of witches. Everyone here knows about it. Most of the locals have something supernatural in their bloodline." Mal smiled. "I'm one-quarter elf."

"Elf?" She started to laugh, only to realize he was serious.

"Lily's boyfriend is a werewolf," he continued.

"I was going to say Polly drugged me, and I need you to please keep an eye on me for signs of hallucinations." She searched his face. "Maybe I need to keep an eye on you."

"Jess?" Lily's excited voice screamed from the other side of the window.

Jesse turned to see her sister rushing down the stairs. Lily wore an oversized flannel shirt, denim jeans, and wool socks. Wavy brown hair was pulled back into a ponytail. She came off the porch onto the drive without shoes. She hopped and waved.

Jesse hurried out of the car to embrace her sister.

"I can't believe you're actually here!" Lily held her tight. "Polly said you wanted to move in."

"Uh…" Jesse started to shake her head.

"No?" Lily's smile fell a little. "So, Polly is just

being Polly. Well, never mind all that. I'm glad you're here. Finally."

"Lily," Mal acknowledged, coming up behind Jesse.

"Oh, hey, Mal," Lily said. "Thank you for bringing her. Polly said you're staying with us tonight?"

"I don't wish to intrude," he denied half-heartedly.

"We're practically a hotel. Everyone intrudes." Lily laughed. "Come on. We have plenty of food left over from dinner. I'll make you a plate."

"A plate?" Jesse arched a brow. "Look at you, all domesticated."

"And profitable," Lily said quietly, hooking Jesse by the arm. "Six months now, in the green. Not trust fund money, *our* money. I can't tell you how good that feels."

"Is Dante here?" she asked.

"He's on a date tonight," Lily said. "I normally don't like when he flirts with the guests, but our brother hasn't had the best of luck with the ladies, so I pretended not to notice this time. Anyway, let me show you around."

Lily pointed toward the mountains. "Mara is at the mining ghost town with some friends, which is that way. They call it Unlucky Valley.

And I do mean ghost town, not just abandoned, but actual ghosts." She then pointed toward the valley. "The town of Lucky Valley is that way. It's much smaller than you're used to in the city, but it grows on you even if the locals don't always."

"What's with all the gnomes?" Jesse glanced along the porch. Their painted eyes seemed to watch her through the railing. "You kind of embraced the whole B&B theme, didn't you?"

"Ignore them. They're nosy. They like to move around, so be sure to lock the bathroom door when you take a shower." Lily pulled her by the arm into the home.

When Jesse bumped the doorframe, energy radiated from the wood like tiny shocks of electricity. She jerked away from the odd sensation.

Lily didn't notice as she chatted about the various rooms and antique furniture. Next to the stairs by the front door was a living room. The gold and red of the velvet couch did not look inviting. Wooden legs were carved into swirling patterns. A stone fireplace stood barren.

A library with striped cushioned chairs and a writing desk held more books than any home Jesse had ever been inside. In the dining room, a stately table set had space for fourteen people. Three of the chairs were occupied by gnome statues. Their pointy hats peaked over the top of the table. Herman tapped across the wood as if dancing for them. Polly clapped her hands, laughing.

Distracted by the show, Jesse nearly tripped on a gnome sitting on a toilet in the middle of the floor.

"You get used to them," Lily said, picking up the toilet gnome and moving him closer to the wall. "They actually make quite good gardeners."

The smell of food came from a back kitchen, luring her in that direction.

"Are you hungry? I just put everything in the fridge, so it shouldn't be too cold yet," Lily said. "I can show you upstairs to a room later."

Jesse nodded. She turned, expecting Mal to be behind her. He wasn't.

A bulldog snored on a dog bed in the corner near a back door in the kitchen. The animal opened one eye to look at her, but the sound didn't stop.

"That's my familiar. Winston." Lily said it like it was completely normal to have a familiar. "If you see a spiteful cat, that's Mara's creature. Stay clear. It has a temper. Much like Mara."

"And Dante said he has a pet raccoon?" Jesse said.

"Familiar," Lily corrected. She reached into

the fridge and started pulling out leftover containers. "Bartholomew. Which I thought was weird at first, but it makes sense when you get to know him."

Lily took out a pan of lasagna.

Jesse nodded. "So you're accepting the whole family of witches thing, aren't you?"

"Not publicly or anything. I don't tell guests." Lily took plates out of the cupboard and started making three servings. "It helps our lives make sense. Haven't you had anything at all strange happen yet?"

Jesse thought of all the strange confessions. "Like what?"

Lily glanced at Winston. "Animal voice in your head?"

Jesse eyed the English Bulldog. She wasn't sure what that squishy fur ball would say. More food? More nap? Rub my belly?

"No." She shook her head.

"How about objects moving?" Lily looked toward the doorway. A gnome statue of a woman in a pointed shower cap had appeared next to the entryway as if to stand guard. She held a towel around her curvy middle and had a surprised expression.

"No."

Lily put a plate in the microwave. "Do you see ghosts?"

"No."

Lily sighed. "So, nothing strange?"

Jesse shrugged. Part of her was so happy to see her sister, but this version of Lily felt different. It was as if Lily had grown up without her. She had a home, a business, a man, a dog. She had a belief in something, even if that something was magic. She seemed...happy.

"Some kids stole my car and set it on fire. Insurance has been a joke," Jesse said, just to have an answer to her sister's questions. "And my kitchen sink exploded this morning. Soaked everything right before I had to go to work. Then Polly showed up and got me fired, drugged me with a potion—at least, I think she did, as I was hallucinating for the entire trip here, which felt like it took a few hours instead of the normal one or two days."

Lily frowned. "Car and sink? Have more things like that been happening? Things that you would chalk up to very bad luck?"

"I haven't exactly been rolling in the good luck," Jesse gave a small laugh, though she really didn't think it was funny. "Someone stole my bank card and went on a shopping spree. I had to fight with the bank to get the charges reversed. It took months, and now I'm behind on bills because of all the late fees."

"Are you okay? Do you need money?" Lily asked, trying to touch Jesse's arm.

"I didn't come for your money." Jesse let her sister touch her, but she didn't like feeling pitied. Actually, she hadn't chosen to come to Lucky Valley at all.

She remembered saying yes when Polly asked her, but she didn't feel like she was in her right mind when she did.

Jesse thought of Mal and the fact that he wanted her to close Marigold's will. "I'm here to sign away whatever it is that Marigold left me in that box. I keep telling them I don't want it. I figured the only way they'll stop harassing me is if I sign some papers."

"How can you say no if you don't know what's in the safe deposit box? Don't you think you owe it to yourself to give this a chance? What is keeping you in Spokane? Your family is here. I'm here. Dante is here. Even Mara. Don't you want to get to know your sister?"

Jessie couldn't say she felt a connection to Mara.

The microwave beeped, and Lily took the food out, only to replace the plate with another. She put a fork and garlic bread next to the lasagna and carried it toward the dining room. Mal sat at the table with Polly, watching Herman's performance. He glanced up at her as she appeared in the entryway from the kitchen. He gave her a slight smile and nodded his head.

Lily placed the plate in front of him and said, "I hope you like Italian."

"Yes, thank you," he answered.

"Herman?" Lily looked at the lobster expectantly. The crustacean tapped his feet on the table in what looked to be excitement. Her sister nodded her head. "Small lasagna, coming right up."

Jesse followed her sister back to the kitchen. "I don't think lobsters eat pasta."

"That one does," Lily laughed. "He has a surprisingly big appetite. I learned not to question it. Herman is as strange as Polly. I think it has to do with all the spells she's cast around him. I think the magical residue has rubbed off or something."

"You look really happy, Lily." Jesse rubbed her sister's arm briefly before pulling away. "I'm glad you found a place where you belong."

"I want you to feel like you belong here too because you do."

"I'm visiting now," Jesse said. She had a few weeks before rent was due to figure something out. It's not like she had to get back to Spokane for a work shift.

"You were so young when mom did what she did." Lily sighed sadly.

"I remember things," Jesse said. "I remember how it affected you and Dante."

"Do you remember Suellen Grace?" Lily asked.

"Our imaginary friend? Yeah. So what? A lot of kids have imaginary friends."

"One that we all could describe the same way. You know she wasn't imaginary," Lily insisted.

The transparent girl had seemed real.

"The flying dolls?" Lily continued.

"I…" Jesse shook her head. "You guys always blamed me for throwing them. That counselor said we were coping with our unstable early childhood living in a car with a mentally unhinged mother. But I never touched them. I might have been messed up, but I was never a liar. Dante was the one always telling stories."

"With everything that you know in mind, doesn't this make sense?"

Jesse glanced around the bed-and-breakfast kitchen.

"This." Lily lifted her hand. Tiny sparks of light came off her fingertips before fizzling out.

Jesse leaped back. Winston lifted his head to watch.

"Magic," Lily said. "Real magic. Don't you want to learn how to use it? Control it?"

Jesse looked at her hand, unable to answer. Nothing in life came free. Magic would have a cost. She wanted normal.

The microwave beeped, and her sister took the second plate out. Lily put in a third dish.

Jesse looked at her sister's hand. Lily showed she wasn't holding anything to have caused sparks before taking a teacup saucer and placing little portions of the heated food onto it for the lobster. Then she carried both plates out for Polly and Herman.

Jesse shied away from the gnome in the doorway as she passed. She purposefully bumped the back of her hand against the entry-way. The flow of electricity rolled from the wood into her hand. This time she didn't jerk away.

"This is delicious," Mal told Lily. "Thank you."

Jesse sat next to him as Lily returned to the kitchen. Her legs shook nervously as if the electricity went down her body.

She watched as Herman examined his small plate. She leaned towards Mal and whispered,

"This is so strange. Don't you think this is strange?"

"Around here, you'll see stranger," he answered, apparently unaffected by seeing a lobster eat lasagna.

"I want to see a happy plate, Herman," Polly said in a voice that sounded like a mother speaking to a small child.

Herman kicked the plate with one of his feet.

"Don't talk back," Polly scolded in a low tone.

"You all right?" Mal whispered while Polly and Herman continued to have their conversation.

"You mean, am I hallucinating?" Jesse shrugged and nodded toward the crustacean. "Logically, the answer to that question would be yes."

"I'm sorry if you feel like we forced you to come. When I came to see you, I never intended to make you come here. I was hoping I could convince you." Mal looked genuinely apologetic.

Something about the deepness of his eyes made her want to trust him. Nothing about this town or this house, or these people was logical. But Lily was right. In a way, it made things from her childhood make sense.

Jesse looked at her hand on her lap and

wiggled her fingers, trying to see if sparkly light would come out of them like Lily's. Nothing did.

"That's not how magic works, pumpkin doodle," Polly said. "You have to have intent and focus, but not think about it."

Jesse glanced up. How did Polly know what she was trying to do?

"Eat up." Lily set a plate of food in front of Jesse before sitting down. "I can't believe you're finally here. I want to hear everything that's been going on with you."

"We talk every week," Jesse said.

"I didn't know about the bad luck," Lily countered. "Why didn't you tell me your bank card was stolen? What else don't I know? Spill."

Jesse took a bite of her food and nodded. "Mm, sis, did you make this? Wow. This is a really good lasagna."

CHAPTER FIVE

JESSE SAT ALONE on the house's front steps, gazing at the stars in the open sky. Lily's boyfriend, Nolan, came to pick her up to deal with a plumbing problem that suddenly sprung up at one of the cabins. He seemed like a nice guy from the two seconds they had to talk. Yet, Jesse couldn't help looking up at the three-quarter moon to make sure he wasn't going to turn into a monster like they did in the movies.

The fresh mountain air had a chill, but she didn't care. As much as Jesse loved seeing her sister, she needed a moment to breathe and think.

"May I join you?" Mal appeared next to her.

Jesse's breath caught in surprise. She'd been so deep into her own thoughts that she hadn't heard him come outside. She turned to look up at him. Lights coming through the windows illuminated his face.

Jesse moved over to allow him to sit next to her.

"Lily seems nice," he said. "I haven't had many chances to talk to her before tonight."

"She's different," Jesse answered.

"How so?"

"She's…" Jesse looked around the beautiful landscape. "Relaxed. Happy."

"That's a good thing."

Mal sat close enough that she could feel his warmth radiating from him. She naturally leaned closer.

"I'm selfish." She sighed, unsure why she admitted as much. "I wanted her to be unhappy here. I wanted her to come back to Spokane."

He nodded, just listening.

"I wanted to be able to point out how crazy this place was, how wrong." Jesse stared at the sky. The shadowy line of the distant mountains cut off the stars. Insects hummed and buzzed to break the silence. "The world feels empty here. In the city, I'm always trying to block other people. Especially lately. They all seem to want something from me, normally an ear to listen to whatever weirdness is on their mind and then for me to tell them what to do about it."

Jesse turned to study him.

"What?" His lips curled a little at the side, drawing her attention.

"Why aren't you telling me about your daddy issues or something?"

He shrugged. "Don't have any. My dad is cool."

"The bully from the third grade?"

"Barnes? We're friends now."

"The waitress who dropped a slice of pizza on your leg and then ran away as the sauce burned your thigh?"

"That's oddly specific." He laughed.

"I like that I feel the silence in you," she said. "Does nothing bother you?"

"Sure, but I don't let those things control me. I fix what I can and settle with the rest." His fingers wrapped hers. She'd been so focused on his smile that she hadn't realized their hands were touching. "You're chilled."

She shook her head in denial. Jesse didn't feel cold. She felt his warmth moving up her arm.

"I have to ask," she whispered.

"Then ask."

"What do elves do?"

He chuckled. "Elf things."

"What are elf things?"

"What are human things? What are witch things?"

"Point taken." Jesse started to pull back.

His grip on her hand tightened. "There are many myths out there, depending on the elfin heritage, but most of it comes from the Medieval period. Some elf communities are said to harm. Others are said to help. But it's like humans. Some human tribes were bad. Some were decent. It comes down to the individual."

"You're good," Jesse said, certain of her assessment.

"I try to be," he said.

"What about magic?"

"We have some," he said. "Nothing like the Crawford and Goode witches, though. Mine tends to help me get through paperwork quickly. And I've got a good memory."

"What about...?"

"About?" he prompted.

"Compatibility." Jesse glanced at his mouth and then back up into his eyes. As soon as she asked, it felt like a very human thing to say. If Lily made it work with a werewolf, surely a human and elf would match. Right?

"I found us to be very compatible when talking on the phone," he said.

"I meant…"

"I know what you meant." Mal leaned forward to kiss her.

Their lips met, and the tingling sensation she had felt when she touched the house's door-frames returned. It worked its way into her mouth. For a moment, they held still as if waiting for the other to pull back or proceed. Slowly, their lips began to move, and the kiss deepened. The tingling magic ran down her neck into her shoulders before dissipating down her body.

She held transfixed in the moment. All worrying thoughts left her.

Mal's hand ran up her arm to cup her face. His thumb slid close to their mouths as he caressed her cheek.

Slowly, she pulled away to look at him.

"Yeah," he whispered. "I'd say we're compatible."

She started to resume the kiss when he suddenly turned his face to the side, stopping her.

"What?" She leaned back in surprise.

"Listen."

Jesse looked over the yard. "I don't hear anything."

"Exactly. The bugs have stopped chirping." Mal took her hand and slowly stood, prompting her to do the same. He kept his eyes on the yard as he stepped backward on the stairs. "Get inside."

"Why?" Jesse searched the shadowy driveway. "I don't see anything."

A chattering noise came from behind the car.

"What is that? A bird?" She started to step forward to take a look.

Mal pulled on her hand, stopping her. He didn't answer.

A second chattering joined the first. A loud *pop* sounded as a tire blew on the car. A corner of the vehicle dropped toward the ground.

Jesse gasped in fright and jumped back. Her heel hit the ledge of the step, and she cried out in pain. A second *pop* followed the first. The chattering turned to strange laughter as the back of the rental car rested lower than before on flat tires. The sound of breaking glass preceded the vehicle rocking back and forth.

"What is that? Ghosts? I don't see anything." Jesse couldn't take her eyes off the car.

"Worse." Mal tugged her back on the steps toward the front door. "Gremlins."

"What?" Jesse frowned, limping.

"They're related to goblins," he said.

The car hood flew open, and three small creatures converged on the engine. Their dark bodies made it difficult to see the details, but she detected pointy ears and claws. They began tearing at the wires and tubes, destroying everything they could manage to rip from inside. A battery flew at them, knocking into the porch rail.

Jesse screamed. Mal pulled her into the house and slammed the door shut, bolting it.

"What's the ruckus?" Polly asked, not appearing too concerned.

The sound of claws scratched the wood and rattled the door.

"Gremlins," Mal answered.

"Who woke them up?" Polly asked. "I thought they were sleeping in an undisclosed mine."

"So did I." Mal went to pull a couch in front of the door to block the entrance.

"Oh, pish." Polly waved her hand. The couch slid away from Mal's grip and returned to its place in the living room. Winston rushed into the room and stared at the wall. "They won't get in. They'll just make a lot of noise. Don't worry. The gnomes will distract them. We can weather this gremlin storm."

Several screeches were followed by loud thuds as the creatures thumped against the siding. *Ahh-thud. Ahh-thud. Ahh-thud-thud.*

Jesse gave a small jump of surprise each time

one of them made contact. A gremlin hit a window, causing the glass to reverberate. The outline of its body showed through the drapes, bordered by a green glow as it slid down the glass.

"See, protected," Polly said, gesturing at the green with a yawn. She disappeared into the dining room. "Come on, Herman. Say good-night to your friends. They need to go outside and take care of the noisy riffraff."

The thuds continued.

Winston leaped up onto the couch and gave a small bark as a shadow passed the window. He stood on the cushion, his entire backside wiggling instead of his tail.

"Yes. Of course, it's her fault, but we can't very well go blaming her for bringing them with her. How was she to know her neglect would wake them up?" Polly said in the other room.

Ahh-thud-thud.

Jesse grabbed hold of Mal's arm for comfort. "This is my fault?"

"No." He tried to give her a reassuring smile.

"But I did this by not coming to check the box sooner?" she insisted.

Thud-rattle-thud.

He didn't answer, but that was answer enough.

"Pumpkin doodle and doodle-dee, you can sleep upstairs, second floor." Polly walked past, holding Herman against her shoulder like a burping baby. "Bedroom with the green door is free. Purple door smells like a flower garden lost a battle against the weeds. But the storage room is available. I don't recommend inside the trunk. That's Bartholomew's play area."

More thuds sounded from the back of the house.

Jesse glanced into the dining room. All of the gnomes were gone.

"There's nothing we can do tonight," Mal said. "The car is destroyed even if we wanted to try to outrun them. They should tire by morning."

Mal kept hold of her hand as they walked upstairs. The pain in her ankle lessened enough that she could ignore it. The thuds remained around the first story as if they couldn't launch their little bodies high enough to hit the second floor.

They found a bathroom door open to reveal a clawfoot tub. Next to it were closed purple and green doors. The smell of dead flowers wafted from one. Mal ignored it and opened the green door. He flipped on the light switch.

"I'll…" He glanced at the purple door. "I'll find a place to sleep. Yell if you need me."

The thuds continued.

Jesse pulled him into the room. "Please don't take this as an advance, but would you mind staying in here tonight? Or at least until—"

Thud.

"Until they stop?" she finished.

Nothing about her life right now was normal. She wasn't some prude, but she also didn't invite guys home on the first date. But did this really compare to a first date? They'd traveled through several states at magical speeds to stay with her witch relatives, and now the house was under attack by gremlins.

"If I'm alone, I'll just listen to that thudding all night, worrying about them getting inside." Jesse rubbed her arms. She lowered to the floor to look under the bed. It was empty. The gremlins were horrible-looking things, little gnarled creatures full of claws and fangs, and she didn't want to imagine them underneath her all night.

Mal quietly closed the door behind him. "I can stay up if you want to try to fall asleep."

Jesse sat on the edge of the bed. "There is enough room on here for both of us."

He didn't move to join her.

Jesse stood and pulled the blankets down. She

grabbed a few of the decorative pillows and made a wall down the middle. "I promise not to get handsy."

"That's not what I'm worried about," he admitted.

"Oh?"

"The elf part of me can easily become attached when I like someone. If this what's happening between us isn't leading to that, then being in here with you is a bad idea for me."

Jesse saw the sincerity in his expression. "I don't normally share what I'm feeling with people, and honestly, I'm not always good at it when I try. My instincts say I can trust you. I like you. I kind of feel like under a goblin attack isn't the best time to make romantic commitments, but I do like you. That's not a promise, but it's the truth."

"Gremlin," he stated.

She swung around to check the room but saw nothing. She gave a small laugh. "That wasn't funny."

"You said goblin. These are gremlins. They're related, but they're technically two different creatures," Mal corrected. "You need to be careful. Beings tend to get insulted if you misidentify them."

"Noted," she said.

Mal walked around to the far side of the bed and sat down.

Jesse put her back to him and pulled off her tennis shoes and socks. "I don't suppose you want to run outside and grab my phone and wallet out of the car before they find them, do you?"

The bed shifted as he stood.

Jesse turned, reaching out toward him. "No, I was kidding. Don't. It's just stuff."

Mal smiled. "Want me to get the light?"

Jesse nodded. She lay down and curled her back against the pillow wall.

He turned off the light, casting the room into shadows. Moonlight trailed through the window, but it took her eyes a moment to adjust. The bed shifted under his weight.

"Thank you for staying with me," she said. "I owe you one."

"Come with me to claim the lockbox tomorrow, and we'll call it even. If that thing is waking up gremlins, I would hate to think what it'll do when it really gets started."

Jesse took a deep breath and nodded. "Yes. I'll get the box. My feelings about keeping the inheritance have not changed, but we can get the box."

His hand found her arm in the darkness, and he squeezed it lightly. "Thank you, Jesse."

"Good night, Mal." She didn't pull away, and neither did he. The pressure on her arm felt as if it kept her steady and safe. The thudding continued but sounded farther away as they hid in the room.

"Night, Jesse."

CHAPTER SIX

Claw marks gouged the wood of the siding as the pieces lay strewn over the yard. Though none of the creatures had breached the house's interior, they did a number on the outside. The home's damage was limited to the bottom half of the Victorian, reaching higher in areas the gremlins had something to launch from, like a birdbath or a railing.

The vandalism wasn't reserved only for the house. Leaves had been shredded from the bushes, and holes had been dug into the yard. They had dented the rental car and tore apart the engine. The wrecked vehicle stood in contrast to Nolan's pickup parked next to it.

Mal pulled Jesse's cellphone and some torn pieces of cash off the floorboard. The device had a cracked screen but still turned on when he pushed the button. He automatically started calculating the cost of the damage to the rental car and the house. The sum wasn't pretty.

"At least we can guess who tore out the plumbing in Cabin Three," Lily was saying from around the side of the house.

"You know I support real work over magical fixes, but in this case, I think we should ask Polly to help us glamor the mess until I can get it done," Nolan answered. Mal knew the man well. As the city's code enforcer, he worked with the law office. "We can't let the guests see it like this. No one is going to believe this was a tornado. They scratched the hell out of it."

Tornados and straight-line winds were two of the most popular excuses used in Lucky Valley. Mal should know. He'd represented more than a few claims against the insurance companies not wanting to pay for damages.

"Whenever she uses that much magic, things get weird around here," Lily countered. "Things were just starting to settle. I mean, we're making a profit, guests are in the cabins, and we finally got those phantom Christmas lights to go away. The gnomes are behaving somewhat."

"My love," Nolan chuckled. "Things are

pretty weird around here right now, and I don't think we can blame it on Polly's visit."

Mal thought about going inside to give them privacy.

"I know," Lily muttered. "It's Jesse. I'm sorry. But she's my sister."

"Nothing to be sorry about." Nolan's voice became softer.

Mal moved closer to keep listening. He couldn't help himself. They were discussing Jesse.

"When I fell in love with you," Nolan continued, "I knew you came with a package of craziness."

"Hey, now!" A light smack sounded in response.

Nolan laughed.

"This isn't funny," Lily protested. "It's just, now the gnomes will get all feisty and emboldened like after the ghost battle. Polly is probably inside, gluing a few of them back together right now. They'll start popping up everywhere and scaring the crap out of all of us. Do you remember with Twinkle Tittle or whatever he's called appeared on the Travers' wedding cake?"

"You have to admit, it was romantically adorable," Nolan said. "He drove that little man statue into a vanilla tomb. The last I saw, he and the bride were living happily together behind the barn."

"You're a..." Lily muttered

"Romantic? Amazingly handsome? Good with a hammer?" Nolan suggested.

"Doofus," Lily finished. "Now, help me think. What about a tornado with claws? Bear-nado? Oh, or how about a tornado picked up one of those old metal windmills and spun it against the house?"

Mal felt a little funny eavesdropping now that they weren't discussing Jesse. He finally showed himself. The couple turned to him in surprise.

"Believe it or not, a tornado with a metal windmill has been used a few times," Mal said.

"Oh, hey." Lily pulled away from where she held onto Nolan's arm. "I didn't hear you come down. Usually, we have coffee ready, but after last night, we only just got back to the house."

"Then you haven't been inside to see the electricity is out." Mal surveyed the damage. "Those gremlins were in top form."

"That's probably what happened to the transformer." Nolan crossed his arms over his chest. "How many?"

"Dozen, at least," Mal said.

Nolan nodded. "Do we know why?"

Mal sighed and looked toward the second story where he'd left Jesse snuggled in bed.

"Right. Jesse's bad luck." Lily sighed. "It was the same for Dante and me when we first started getting our magic. It didn't stop or at least lessen until we accepted who we are. I don't know if Jesse will ever accept it. Polly practically had to trick her into coming."

"She's agreed to go with me today to open the box," Mal said. "She doesn't want what's inside, but then…"

"Who knows what Marigold left inside." Lily rubbed her temples.

The lights inside the house flickered and turned on. Lily turned her attention upwards, prompting Mal and Nolan to do the same.

"Well, the phantom lights are back," Lily grumbled. "Polly must have started her cleanup spells."

A string of what looked like forgotten fairy lights draped over the side of the house. They emitted a soft glow, but when he looked closely, they appeared to be transparent.

"Coffee?" Lily asked.

"Yes, please," Nolan answered.

"Give me five minutes." Lily went around the side of the house, and they heard the front door open.

"I thought the gremlins were hibernating in one of the old mines," Nolan said. "I checked the sealed exit myself. Who opened it? Who would even know where to find it?"

Mal didn't answer. He wouldn't have been able to find the entrance without a map, and it's not like the locations of monster hideaways were lying around for anyone to check out.

"You know who they're going to blame," Nolan insisted. "Lily will never say it, but she's been working so hard to get the town to accept the Goode family—not that the town necessarily deserves her kindness after how they act around her and her brother."

"Convince her it's the right idea to let Polly hide the evidence of this mess," Mal said. "With luck, we'll figure out how to lure the gremlins back into their hole before anyone else finds out they're wreaking havoc. People will be much less frightened of strands of rogue ghost lights than angry monsters destroying the city."

"And you convince Jesse to accept her responsibilities as a member of this family," Nolan countered, on the defensive. Though, knowing he was a hot-blooded werewolf close to a full moon helped Mal ignore the attitude. "I will not watch Lily's life be destroyed by more of Marigold's magic."

Mal wondered just how much sway they thought he had on Jesse. Sure, they'd had a few deep telephone conversations and technically spent the night together, but that hardly put him in a position of authority. In fact, he doubted anyone would ever be in a place of authority over Jesse. Her independence was what he loved about her.

"Crap," Mal muttered, letting his head drop forward.

"What?" Nolan demanded in concern.

Mal shook his head. "Never mind. I just remembered something I forgot to do."

He'd forgotten to safeguard his heart from this very thing. Love? The word had just slipped into his thoughts, but there was no denying the truth of it. He'd fallen in love with her from the first time he saw her picture in that damned legal file at the office before he even dialed her phone number.

"Jesse's going for the box today," Nolan said. A mate-possessive werewolf close to the full moon would be even more temperamental than usual. "That's the only work that matters."

"I hear you, buddy," Mal said, keeping his tone even and non-threatening. "Jesse loves her siblings. She'll do right by them. I promise."

"Is that your elf talking?" Nolan asked. "You've sensed her intentions?"

"Yes." Mal nodded. "She can be trusted."

Nolan seemed to relax some. "Coffee? I have camping gear we can use while we wait for the power to turn back on."

Mal was slower to follow as the werewolf went into the house. Nolan only thought of gremlins and reputations, but Mal knew so much more than that was at stake now. He loved Jesse and would do anything to ensure she survived whatever was coming.

CHAPTER SEVEN

"YOU KNOW you don't have to do this. Say the word, and I'll drive you home. Right now. Today."

Jesse looked at Mal in surprise. "Your firm has been begging me for months, *years*, to take care of this safe deposit box. Now I agree to do it, and you're trying to usher me out of town. What gives, Mal?"

"I didn't know what I was asking." He kept his tone low as he pulled her deeper into the library for privacy. "We were concerned about magic leaking out of the box, but if it summoned up gremlins, or lured them, or woke them up, whatever it is that went on, then who knows what will happen if we open it all the way? Perhaps we can seal it in a bigger vault. Iron perhaps.

Encased in steel. There has to be something that can contain it."

Jesse went to the window and looked at the destruction on the front lawn. "You want me to leave Lily and Dante with this mess? My mess? I might not have chosen it, but Marigold dropped this on me. They didn't abandon me when we were little, sleeping in a car. They were just kids themselves cleaning up Marigold's mess. I'm not abandoning them now when it's my turn to protect them."

It wasn't just living in a car. It was being left in the cold without food. Lily and Dante had scrounged for scraps and always fed her first. They didn't think she remembered as much as she did, and she would never tell them otherwise. They seemed happy to think she'd forgotten the worst of it. But Jesse remembered the feeling of hunger. She remembered that fear pressing in on the window in panted breaths from toothless grins. She remembered seeing things a child should never have to see within those dank alleys.

In many ways, Marigold abandoning them had been the kindest thing she could have done. Because she absolutely sucked at being a mother.

"I'm going." Jesse looked through the glass for signs of the creatures. "Are they gone?"

"Yes, I was just out there," Mal answered, placing his hand on her shoulder.

She drew comfort from his touch, just as she had when he lay in the bed on the other side of the pillow wall.

"The sooner, the better," Jesse determined. "I want it to be over. I don't want to think about it. I don't want to talk myself out of it. Let's open that stupid box and be done with it once and for all."

"Great. We'll go now," Nolan said behind them.

Jesse turned to see Lily's boyfriend in the archway. Nolan had always been friendly enough during their video calls, but seeing him in person gave her a whole new perspective. She'd imagined him as a manly man contractor, a working-class man who labored hard and liked watching sports on television. Knowing he was a werewolf didn't exactly tamp down her impression of him. She felt an energy coming off him, something restless and wild that was held back with a tiny ribbon of control.

But she also felt that Nolan loved her sister and wanted nothing more than to make her happy. Those two things meant everything.

"I need to borrow a change of clothes from

Lily," Jesse said, looking at the work uniform she'd slept in. "I'm not dressed for a bank visit."

Mal exhaled what sounded to be a small laugh and said wryly, "You might be for this bank."

"Still, I want a shower." Jesse moved toward the hall that would take her to the kitchen. "Lily in the kitchen?"

Nolan nodded but didn't move out of the way to let her pass to the hallway. "You shower. I'll have her bring you something."

Jesse sensed he was eager to get this done and didn't insist on talking to Lily herself. She made her way up the stairs. She took a shaky breath when she was alone on the top landing. Fear rolled into her at the thought of what she had to do—fear of the unknown, fear of facing what people thought was her destiny, fear of being torn open by angry gremlins.

CHAPTER EIGHT

Unlucky Valley Ghost Town

Jesse stood on the dirt street of the abandoned ghost town that time forgot. Once a thriving mining village, Old Lucky Valley had fallen prey to the infamous bad luck.

Lily had started to tell her the family history more than once, but Jesse had always cut her off. Standing in the middle of the empty town covered in dust and raw, sun-bleached wood, she wondered if she should have paid more attention.

Polly strolled over a boarded sidewalk in front of old businesses, talking to herself and pausing to stare into empty doorways. Only some of the place names could be read through the faded paint on the signs and storefronts.

Mal had jogged ahead to meet with someone at the bank. Jesse followed behind at a slower pace as she tried not to get too close to any of the buildings. The center of the street felt the safest as she'd at least see something coming at her.

"So, was this town the Goodes' or the Crawfords'?" Jesse asked Lily. Her sister was several paces away, and she had to speak loudly to make her voice carry.

"Both." Mara appeared from inside a building wearing sweatpants and a jacket. The bandana around her head gave off a Rosie the Riveter vibe. She ran her hand along the stone-and-wood siding of the saloon before hopping off the wooden sidewalk onto the dirt street. "What are you doing here? I thought you didn't like any of this."

"I'm here to make a bank withdrawal," Jesse answered, not liking Mara's aggressive tone. So, this was her baby sister Lily kept trying to tell her about—the half-demon baby with a penchant for lying.

"Mara," Lily rushed forward, "I'm so happy you and Jesse can finally meet."

Lily put herself between the two women like a human shield. Mara didn't look like her siblings. Her hair was a darker shade, her eyes pure brown, and her face heart-shaped. Jesse thought maybe it was because Mara was technically a Crawford but not a Goode since they had different fathers.

Mara sighed. "Bank's this way."

"The Crawfords and the Goodes founded this town in the 1800s," Lily said to answer Jesse's question. "So, both sides."

"It was a refugee camp," Mara corrected, almost irate. "Don't throw a dress on a pig and try to make it the belle of the ball. No one had anywhere to go, so they all landed here. Jedediah Crawford just happened to be the first to trip over a gold nugget. The Goodes already had money from who knows what. They looked at each other and said, well, you're rich, we're rich, let's get richer together, and a pact was formed."

"Refugees?" Jesse looked at Lily for an explanation.

"Supernaturals who had been run out of Europe," Lily said.

Jesse nodded. "And when she says pact, she doesn't mean—"

"*She*," Mara interrupted, "means what she said. They formed a pact, a contract, a covenant. Some locals say the devil was there, but they might just be pissed about the whole mine-collapsing-and-killing-a-hundred-and-eighteen-workers thing."

"The way I heard it," Lily resumed in a softer tone. "The Goodes got greedy. The Crawfords weren't careful with worker safety. The two families stopped getting along. Think Hatfields-and-McCoys type feuding, but with magic and more ego. It started small, magic was used, it escalated, and finally ended in crops dying of some disease, a church burning down, and the mine collapse, all within a three-day period."

"Every family in town lost at least one member that day," Mara said. "But the worst part is, they didn't all have to die. The Goodes and Crawfords couldn't get their act together long enough to agree on a rescue plan, and by not working together, bye-bye miners."

"The locals blamed our ancestors, and thus the bad luck curse was born," Lily said. "I don't necessarily think it's fair that our family is blamed for building fires, bad crops, and a mining accident during an era where safety standards consisted of carrying a caged bird into the tunnels to see if the air was clean."

Jesse frowned. "I don't know, Lily. It sounds like our ancestors should shoulder some of that blame."

"And then came Marigold," Mara drawled. "Dear ol' Mom, marrying Joseph Goode and stirring ancient business that shouldn't have been stirred. They gave the curse a whole new life. Then he died and left this place to Marigold. We all know how well Marigold handled responsibilities. But he neglected to leave her access to the trust funds to take care of it."

Joseph Goode died in a car wreck when Lily, Dante, and Jesse were very young. Jesse didn't know her father. Though she didn't appreciate Mara speaking ill of him, she didn't know enough to defend him either.

"Nolan said our mom used to wander around town looking like death warmed over, scaring children." Lily tried to lead Jesse toward the shaded sidewalk, but Jesse refused to leave the dirt road. "They used to say, 'Stay away from Marigold Crawford Goode, or she'll steal your soul and leave you wandering.'"

"Lovely," Jesse muttered wryly.

"Right?" Mara said with a nod of agreement.

"Great. Trust that you two would bond over sarcasm," Lily sighed in exasperation.

Jesse shrugged. "I learned it from you."

Mara laughed.

The sound of the sidewalk creaking caught her attention, and Jesse watched Polly skip along the wooden planks. A garden gnome with a blue hat and a sheriff's star badge stood with hands hovered over pistols in front of what could have been a police station.

"What is with Polly leaving these gnomes everywhere?" Jesse asked.

"They're her friends. And she doesn't leave them. They get themselves where they're going," Lily answered. Her sister again tried to lure her toward the buildings. "I thought you'd like exploring a ghost town."

Jesse eyed the area where Mal had disappeared. She didn't want to spend more time than necessary inside. "Sure, if they didn't actually come with reports of ghosts who hate every relative on our family tree."

With each step, the feeling of dread increased inside of her.

"Don't be a baby," Mara said. "I camp out here all the time. I slept here last night. Between the miners and the townsfolk currently calling Unlucky Valley's spectral plane home, if someone wants to hurt you, they'll find a way to hurt you."

"It's true. She does spend the night here." Lily pointed toward the sheriff gnome. "When I first met her, she was camping in a jail cell."

"I thought you said she was camping with friends. Where are the other people?" Jesse asked.

"Ghosts are my friends," Mara said. "My dad is from here. Well, ghost dad, anyway. The traveler he possessed to seduce Mom. I have no clue where that guy is from."

Mara stared at her as if she expected Jesse to judge her. No, she was *daring* Jesse to judge her.

"Sounds rough," Jesse said instead, not saying any of the thoughts in her head.

"Thanks." Mara nodded as if Jesse had passed some test. "It was."

"So are the ghosts here now, or do they go out adventuring?" Jesse looked around, trying to see anything that appeared out of the ordinary.

"Dante and Polly put a binding spell on this town to keep the ghosts inside," Lily said.

"They possessed me and tried to get me to lead them on an attack of the bed-and-breakfast," Mara added.

"Was a little more than tried, pickle," Polly yelled, clearly eavesdropping though she skipped quite a bit away from them.

Mal appeared from within the bank and waved at her to join him. The building had a weathered stone front and seemed more secure than most of the others.

An older gentleman in a three-piece suit stood beside him, clutching a worn manilla folder.

"Is that a...?" Jesse stared at the old-fashioned suit.

"Uptight banker," Mara answered. "Much scarier than ghosts."

The banker looked at Jesse, Lily, and Mara as they approached. "Miss Jessamine Rosemary Goode?"

"Jesse," Jesse corrected. "That's me."

"This is Alexander Pulsipher," Mal introduced. "He's been in charge of the bank annex here for nearly sixty years."

"Come inside, please," Alexander instructed.

"Why would a bank keep anything of value out here?" Jesse asked, glancing around for signs of trouble before stepping into the old bank. "Why not move it into town?"

Alexander cleared his throat and ducked his head. He and Mal walked around teller cages toward a back office where a giant vault door dominated a wall. Dust coated everything but a path where feet had recently traveled. Jesse covered her mouth and nose while suppressing a sneeze.

"This is the last item remaining at the annex," Alexander said. "I can tell you that the bank will be happy to have it off the books and to revert the office property back into your family trust."

Wires came from the ceiling and coiled on the floor before feeding into a series of cameras around the room, all pointing at the vault. They also powered a floodlight pointed at the door.

"What the…?" Lily looked up.

"I haven't been in this room before," Mara said.

Mal gestured at the wires. "Solar power."

"Yes, we found it necessary to install a security system," Alexander said. "When, um, other measures began showing signs of failure. But I think you can agree that we upheld our end of the bargain. Now, if you wouldn't mind signing some papers, Miss Jessamine—ugh, *Jesse*—I'll get out of here and give you your privacy."

Alexander grabbed a pen from his front suit pocket and flipped open his folder. He tried to hand the pen to Jesse.

She didn't take it as she went to touch the vault door. "How old is this thing?"

"Late 1800s, miss, I believe." Alexander again tried to hand her the pen.

Jesse took it but then pressed her hands against the door. "Can you open it?"

"As soon as you sign." He thrust the paperwork at her.

"Don't you need my driver's license or something?" Jesse asked. "So, you know I am who I say I am?"

"Mr. Rhodes has assured me you are who you say you are." Alexander tapped his folder. "I just need one signature. Right here."

"Jesse." Mal nodded toward the banker.

"Oh, yeah, sure." Jesse glanced at the form before signing it. It basically said she was claiming the box from the bank and releasing them of their duty to safeguard it.

"I can still turn down the will, though, right?" she asked Mal.

He nodded.

"Okay, good." Jesse signed the man's paper.

Before her pen was even lifted, Alexander jerked the file back and sighed as if a giant weight had been lifted off him. He gave a small laugh and fumbled inside his vest pocket to procure an antique key and a weathered paper.

"The code." Alexander handed both items to her. "Pleasure doing business with you. I officially resign as the caretaker. I will now vacate the property."

"Hey, what about your cameras?" Mara asked.

"Keep them," Alexander said. "The bank no longer requires them."

"Sweet." Mara went to check out one of the cameras. "I call dibs."

"Is it time?" Polly's voice came from the bank lobby.

Alexander mumbled something, but the words were lost in the sound of his running footsteps.

"Should we wait for Dante?" Lily asked.

Jesse had yet to see her brother.

Polly tilted her head and looked around the bank office. "No."

Jesse waited for her aunt to follow the answer with a little dance or line of gibberish, but her tone was flat, and she didn't embellish. That in itself didn't make her feel at ease.

Jesse took the large key and shoved it into a matching hole. She turned it and heard a series of mechanical clicks. When she touched the large handle and tried to thrust it up and to the side to open the vault, she felt the same tingling from when she'd touched Lily's doorframes. She jerked her hand back and shook it.

"Entering new rooms is always tricky," Polly said. "But it has to be done, or you'll never escape the one you're in."

"Do you want me to do it?" Mal offered.

"I…" Jesse nodded. She leaned to watch the

seam of the vault door for when he pulled it open.

Mal reached for the handle. A yellow flash of light erupted at the contact, and he was thrust back into one of the cameras. The device crashed to the floor as he managed to right himself.

"Hey! I called dibs. Those are mine. Be careful," Mara protested. "Do you know how much this stuff is worth?"

"Mara," Polly scolded. "Not now."

"Mal, are you all right?" Jesse rushed to him. He trembled as she held his arms.

Mal nodded. "Sorry, I don't think it'll let me open it for you."

"What if I wanted to start a ghost-hunting business with them?" Mara said to Polly.

"Oh!" Polly instantly brightened. "*Polly and Mara's Positively Hauntingly Mystical Magical Ghost-Hunting Experience.*"

"Never mind." Mara shook her head.

Jesse made sure Mal was on his feet before she went back to the door. Taking the handle, she ignored the buzzing in her fingertips as she pushed the handle up. Another mechanical sound reverberated from inside. Jesse pulled, but it didn't budge.

"It's stuck." Jesse tried harder.

"Read the passcode," Polly said.

Jesse looked at the paper Alexander had given her. "Seriously? The passcode is *open*."

Yellow erupted over the metal door as the vault began to creak. The door moved on its own, swinging open to allow her entrance. The floodlight pierced into the darkness, casting thick shadows.

"What did you expect it to say?" Polly asked. "Open sesame?"

"I think it's open says me," Mal said.

"Neither. I figured it'd be in Latin or a dead language," Jesse countered.

"Why? Do you speak Latin or a dead language?" Polly asked.

"No." Jesse peeked inside what appeared to be an old empty vault. The dust had not made it into the safe. The only light was from the bank office.

"Then why would someone leave you a note in those languages?" Polly shook her head. "You're such a silly dilly."

Jesse touched the vault doorframe as she inched inside the room. The energy had lessened. Another camera was on the vault floor. Its broken pieces were pushed into a corner as if swept there with a foot and then abandoned.

On a table in the middle sat an iron box with

a thick bolt slid into a barrel lock. When she stepped closer, she felt as if waves of energy pulsed from within.

"I don't want to do this," she whispered.

Mal appeared beside her.

"You shouldn't be here," she said. "What if it throws you again?"

He took her hand in his. "I'm with you. Whatever you decide. If you stay, I stay. If you go, I'll drive."

Jesse found comfort in him. She remembered having that same sense each time he called to talk about the will. Most of the time, they'd never really ended up talking about it.

"We're right here," Lily said from the door.

Jesse reached forward to pull the bolt. The shock of electricity became almost painful. She bit the inside of her lip, forcing her hand to remain where it was. Every logical part of her brain screamed at her to run. She'd been resisting this moment for a very long time.

Metal scraped on metal as she pulled the bolt. The noise seemed loud in the silence.

Jesse glanced at Mal. He nodded. She felt more than saw his worry, but he didn't leave her side. No one spoke.

Ding. Ding-ding. Da-ding-da-ding-ding.

Jesse gasped at the sudden noise and jerked her hand back. The bolt fell on the floor.

"Sorry, that's Dante's ringtone," Lily said, pulling her phone from her pocket. She stepped away from the door into the office, "Hey, Dante? Where the hell have you been? I've been trying to call you. Jesse's here."

"Oh, I need to talk to him," Polly said, chasing after Lily. "Ask him if he's seen Mr. Wiggle Wabbles."

The sound of a light scuffle came from the office as Polly and Lily fought over the phone.

"Hold on. Talk to Polly. I have to get back——" Lily said.

"What's in there?" Mara prompted.

Jesse flicked the latch forward and flung the lid back. A soft yellowy reflection caught the light from the floods behind her. She slowly leaned forward to look inside.

"What is that?" Mal whispered next to her.

A piece of rock with thick yellow veins sat on a cushion. It was the size of a baseball.

"Gold nugget?" Jesse reasoned with a small laugh of surprise. "Gah, I thought it was going to be some kind of gremlin egg or something."

"Gold? Seriously?" Mara sounded disappointed.

"Well, this was a mining town," Mal said.

"It's just a stupid gold rock," Mara announced to Lily. "False alarm."

"Lily, Dante needs to talk to you," Polly said. "It's urgent."

Jesse reached inside to lift the nugget. "All this hype over—"

The second she made contact, yellow light shot out of the rock and zapped up her arm like lightning. She tried to scream, but her voice locked in her throat.

"Don't touch whatever's inside," Polly said belatedly, sounding closer as if she'd walked into the room. "Oh, well, that's a mippity-mess."

"Jesse?" Mal grabbed hold of her arm. When he touched her, the awareness of him filled her. The energy rush changed directions to flow toward him and launched him away from her body with a bright spark.

Her vision yellowed, and for a moment, she saw into everyone around her. Their emotions, fears, and thoughts all overwhelmed her.

Mara had lived a life of humiliation and fear, locked in a barn like a dirty family secret with only ghosts to play with. But spirits made for bad babysitters, and they'd possessed her body to walk around as human.

Polly's thoughts were much like her speech— a mishmash of disorganization. The vastness of her magical knowledge would take decades to sift through, like a card catalog filed out of order and written in gibberish.

Lily loved Nolan, and that love scared her. She tried to hide it, but the constant fear was there of Nolan leaving. Because to Lily, everyone she loved left her. First, their father. Then their mother. Then Jesse.

Jesse had not realized how her refusal to come to Lucky Valley had hurt her sister. She hadn't meant for it to. Lily never guilted her over it, but she had hurt her deeply.

Most surprising was Mal. His intentions were honorable. He worried for the town about what this box meant. He'd seen video footage of the contents leaking out like dark shadows. He believed that it could be the destruction of New Lucky Valley or a triggering of the old mining town curse. At the same time, he hadn't wanted her to risk herself to open it.

Behind all this, she felt a warmth. It radiated from him into her. There was love there. She saw him staring at her picture. She heard the memory of someone telling him to be careful. That he could lose his heart and never get it back, so he better choose well.

He loved her.

Jesse held onto that feeling, letting it draw her

back to reality. The yellow faded, and she found herself kneeling on the bank vault floor.

"Jesse?" Lily asked, kneeling beside her. "Talk to me."

"Lily!" Dante's voice sounded far away as it came from the phone. "Lily!"

"Mal?" Jesse dropped the gold and turned to look for him. He sat propped up against the vault wall holding the back of his head.

"Are you all right?" Mal reached for her, blinking heavily.

The lingering of his emotions stirred within her. Without thinking, she took hold of his face and kissed him. Jesse realized the feelings were not just one-sided. Those few moments she'd been magically linked to him were like a lifetime of knowledge.

"Whoa, Jesse," Lily teased, sounding a little surprised.

"Get a room," Mara added.

"Lily!" Dante's voice insisted, panicked. "Pick up!"

Jesse turned to see what was happening.

Lily chuckled and lifted the phone. "Everything's fine. Your little sister is making out with..." Her expression fell. "Slow down. I can barely hear you. Let me go outside for better reception."

Polly crossed to the box and pulled out a rolled piece of paper tucked along the cushioned padding. "You always read the card before you open the gift."

Polly tossed it at her.

Jesse caught the paper and unrolled it. She looked at the strange words. "This looks like Latin."

"Well, you don't expect an ancient spell to be in English, do you?" Polly clucked her tongue.

"I don't speak Latin," Jesse insisted.

"Won't do you any good now to read it after you opened your present." Polly sighed. "You kids are always in a hurry."

"What happened?" Mara asked Polly. "Did Jesse get her magic?"

"Jesse already had magic," Polly said. "She hasn't been using it, but she has it."

"I feel…" Jesse rubbed her temple. Her skin crawled as if everyone touched her at the same time, but no one did.

"Hungry?" Polly asked. "I could use a cheeseburger."

"Same," Mara said.

Jesse shook her head and took a deep breath. "I feel…"

"Oh, a game!" Polly clapped her hands and

began shooting off answers. "Happy? Tacky? Slimy? Motion sick?"

Jesse shook her head.

"Invaded?" Polly suggested.

Jesse nodded. That was the closest word so far.

Polly frowned. "Well, that wasn't a very good game. Too easy. Anyone up for Clue?"

Mal pushed to his feet. He reached to touch her face but let his hand fall before making contact. He looked at the gold nugget on the floor. "What happened? What is in that nugget? How is this compared to Pandora's box?"

Polly furrowed her brow at him.

"It's a gold nugget? Money ruins people?" Mal questioned. "Is that what you meant? By giving Jesse gold, it's some kind of spell or lesson? Greed is the ruination of—"

"Knowledge is a great power," Polly interrupted with a wave of her hand to stop his guessing. "Plus, this particular gift can cause one heck of a headache."

Jesse nodded. Her temple was throbbing. "Yes, headache."

"So what is with the nugget?" Mal insisted.

"Her inheritance," Polly answered.

"Which is…?" Mal prompted.

"We don't like to let this knowledge magic

out too much," Polly explained, "but every so often, it grows too strong to be contained, and someone is chosen who needs to carry it around and fizzle it out before we can cram it back into its box. Jesse's magic is a perfect fit. People are already comfortable talking to her and—"

Lily charged into the vault. "Gremlins are in town. We have to go. Dante is holed up with others in the diner, and things are turning nasty. No one can get ahold of Sheriff Tillens."

"Jesse, you're up, pumpkin doodle," Polly said. "You didn't read the note and reverse the damage before taking on your inheritance from that box. This is your battle."

"What?" Jesse shook her head. "No."

"Then they eat your brother," Polly said. "We all have choices, some we choose, and some choose us, but they all have to be made in the end."

"Jess, please," Lily begged. "It's Dante."

Jesse nodded and chose to follow her sister. No matter how scary the threat looked, she couldn't abandon her brother.

"What about the gold?" Mara asked.

"I'll clean up," Polly said. "You kids have fun!"

"Don't touch my cameras," Mara warned. "They're mine."

CHAPTER NINE

"I DON'T FEEL WELL." Jesse leaned her head against the glass as she rode in the passenger seat of Nolan's truck.

Lily drove like a madwoman. The tires skidded on dirt as she took turns too fast. Mal and Mara were squished in the middle as they all crowded in. Mal's arm was around Jesse's shoulders as if trying to help keep her steady as they bounced around.

"Magic is about intent," Lily said, not for the first time. "Just know what you want."

"I want to lay down," Jesse said, closing her eyes. Polly's guess for motion sickness had come too early.

"I still want a cheeseburger," Mara added.

Jesse felt a wave of frustration wash over her. Lily wanted sisters who took things seriously.

"I *am* taking this seriously," Jesse said. "Dante is in trouble, and I have no idea how to stop gremlins, but here I am. I've been screaming at the apparent void for the last two years that I didn't want anything from the inheritance, but here I am. I didn't want to open the migraine box, yet here I am with a pounding head. So, you can stop poking at me."

"I didn't poke," Lily muttered.

"And give Mara a break," Jesse continued. "She's clearly worried about Dante. After the horror show of her childhood, we're lucky she only uses humor to deflect when she's scared. You and Dante are the only family she has ever really known, at least the only ones who care if she lives or dies. Polly, too, but she's such a noodle that she doesn't evoke trust in our baby sis."

"Hey," Mara protested. "Don't talk for me. I never said any of that."

Jesse groaned and dropped her forehead against her arm as she leaned into the door. "Yes, thank you, Mal. You can do something for me. You can rub the back of my neck."

"Are you hearing voices?" Mara asked. "Your boyfriend didn't say anything."

Jesse lifted her head to glance at him.

Mal shook his head and lifted his hand to rub her neck. "But I was thinking it."

Jesse's head fell back down as he massaged her. She kept her eyes closed and stated, "Yes, I suppose I would like you to be my boyfriend."

Mal cleared his throat, and his hand stopped for a moment before resuming.

"I can deduce you didn't say that out loud either," Jesse mumbled. "Why are you all in my head?"

That no one had an answer for.

Jesse focused on her breathing as the truck sped along. She heard the clink of pebbles kicking up from the tires and the creak of the pickup as it rocked back and forth. She found comfort in the meditative simplicity. The headache began to fade.

"Hold on," Lily ordered.

The truck swerved. The motion forced Jesse's head up. They passed through a residential neighborhood.

"This is Lucky Valley?" Jesse asked, staring at the row of white houses with black trim. They all looked like decorated variations of the same cookie-cutter set. One house had red curtains in the windows, another yellow. The flowerpots varied, as did the toys in the yard. One had a porch swing, another a tire swing, and yet another had a hammock in the side yard.

"Yes," Mal answered.

"It looks…" Jesse frowned, a little disappointed. She'd built it up inside her head to be a mythical place. "Normal."

"It is normal," Mal answered. "Supernaturals are just like humans, with different inherited gifts."

Lily snorted, and the vehicle sped up.

"Yeah. *Gifts*," Mara drawled.

"I just thought it would be more Halloweeny." Jesse furrowed her brow.

Lily turned the truck. The tires screeched a little against the road.

The idealistic neighborhood became an apocalyptic landscape as they drove down Main Street. Metal light posts were sliced open with claw marks as if creatures had swung around them in circles. A few were ripped open so badly that they had tipped over.

Cars had crashed into each other, and a few even into the sides of buildings. Their dented hoods and tops reminded her of the rental in Lily's driveway. The doors to a sedan hung open, revealing claw marks on the seats.

Jesse felt a wave of guilt. Was she responsible for unleashing this?

Lily slowed to dodge the cars, driving onto the curb before stopping and shutting off the engine. They peered out of the windows, not seeing anyone.

"Do you think they're gone?" Mara whispered.

"Come on." Lily opened the truck door and climbed out. She reached into the cab, grabbed Mara's arm, and pulled her out. She then waved at Mal and Jesse. "Let's go. Now."

Jesse shivered as her feet hit the pavement. Mal pulled her behind him as they moved across the street. Faces pressed against a diner window beneath a sign that read *Stammerin' Eddie's*.

"Open up," Lily yelled as she reached for the handle. She jerked, but a bearded man on the other side held tight and refused to let them in.

Mal joined Lily at the door. "Paul! Open it!"

"Dante!" Lily yelled. "Are you in there?"

Jesse detected the sound of pattering feet and turned toward the street. Dark images blurred like a converging storm. The sound of tires popping preceded the broken-down vehicles lowering on their flat tires. She felt a rush of anger like a tidal wave coming to pull her under.

Paul must have released the door because she heard a shopkeeper's bell jingle. Someone grabbed her arm and dragged her into the diner. She stood at the door, watching as the gremlins destroyed everything within their reach. They jerked on wires, dented metal, and pulled parts of the engine to throw them on the ground.

"Why did you let them in here?" a man demanded. "We should throw them all out. They caused this. Let them deal with it."

"Yeah, throw them out," a woman agreed.

The aggression and fear were so palpable that they choked Jesse's throat. They were serious. They wanted the Goodes gone. The fear was ingrained in them from generations of blaming everything bad that happened on a curse.

Jesse watched as someone locked the door. They collectively stepped back as the diners stared out the window like they were watching a drive-in movie.

"Try not to move," someone whispered. "Maybe they'll go away like last time."

Jesse didn't think the creatures were planning on leaving. They seemed to be searching for something.

"Jesse?" A hand pressed against her shoulder and forced her around. Dante instantly pulled her into a hug. "Why didn't you tell us you were coming? I wouldn't have gone out if I'd known. Or at least, I would have come home."

"Is she a keeper?" Jesse asked, torn between listening to him and watching the threat outside.

"My date?" Dante shook his head. "No. We had fun, but she left for Maryland this morning."

Jesse turned her full attention back to the door to watch the destruction. How was she supposed to stop this? Why did she agree to come here? This wasn't her world. She was an unemployed waitress with mommy issues.

"Do you think they'll come in here?" Jesse asked.

"I don't know," Dante whispered. "I don't know what they want."

What should she do?

How could she help?

Fight or flight, Jesse thought.

She searched the diner for a safe place to hide. A counter with barstools had been abandoned. Cups of coffee and half-eaten dinners still lined the place settings. The rectangular dining room stretched to the side, long and skinny. Red booths bolted to the black-and-white checkered floor, fixtures hanging from the shiny silver ceiling, and the 1950s tin signs boasting fresh coffee and happy families didn't offer much in the way of protection.

However, it would give the gremlins many things to dent and destroy.

A distraction, maybe? While they got everyone out of a back door?

Was there a back door?

Behind the bar, standard diner equipment was lined up along a short wall. The old-fashioned soda fountain, heat lamps, blenders, and soft serve ice cream machine might make for good projectiles if they had to fight.

Or perhaps the giant coffee maker could scald if they threw the hot liquid?

"I heard you talking. I've never been to Maryland." A woman with auburn hair and rectangular plastic glasses pushed Mal out of her way so she could stand close to Jesse. Her red polo waitress uniform had the name Sal embroidered on it. "I can't remember ever wanting to go there. It's one of those places you never think about. Paris, though, I've wanted to go there and get fat on cheese and croissants. But I know it will never happen. Life has decided to trap me here."

"I was trapped in a well when I was a kid," Paul, the bearded man who had blocked the door said, crowding closer to inch Sal out of the way. "I jumped in. I thought it would be like that television show where the dog comes and saves the boy. I never told anyone I did it on purpose."

"I've never told anyone I wanted to be a

ballet dancer," said a burly man in a cook's grease-stained apron.

The confessions kept coming, the words overlapping as those in the diner tried to talk over each other. They seemed more concerned with telling her things than what was happening in the street.

"I've never…"

"I haven't told…"

"That's nothing. When I was little…"

"What the hell is going on?" Dante thrust his body in front of hers.

"Everyone back," Mal ordered, shoving the bearded man away as he came beside Jesse.

"Please, I don't know how to tell my sister I don't want to keep our mother's house. It smells like mothballs, and I hate it. I've already talked to a realtor," a woman with short black hair tried to tell Jesse. She bounced up and down, trying to see over the crowd.

The sister jerked her down as she tried to hop up. "You did what? You said you agreed with me!"

Suddenly the crowd surged toward Jesse as one sister pushed the other into the cluster.

Jesse cried out as her hip hit the door lock. The shopkeeper's bell jingled. The sound of outside destruction suddenly stopped as the diner erupted into chaos. Dante was jerked into the throng. Someone tried to grab Jesse, but Mal leaped in front of her, only to be shoved into her back.

Jesse's face pressed into the glass. She felt as if their emotions choked her—fear, anger, repression, aggression, denial, longing. They all flowed to congest the air. She grabbed her throat, trying to breathe. Dizziness threatened her consciousness. Desperate to escape, she fumbled for the latch but couldn't get it to open.

A surge of warm yellow light thrust out of her chest, and she suddenly found herself standing alone on the sidewalk. She pulled at her neckline and took several deep breaths.

The locked diner doors rattled violently.

"Jesse!" Mal yelled, his voice muffled. "Jesse!"

Jesse heard low chittering and slowly turned to look behind her. The gremlins had stopped their destruction as they ambled toward her. They hopped off cars and came out of tattered landscaping containers.

"Hello," she tried to speak, lifting her hands to keep them calm. "Easy there."

She automatically started retreating toward the diner, back to safety. But then she heard the rattling doors and knew the people inside were terrified. When she glanced at them, Dante, Lily, and Mal were trying to get out while everyone else tried to stop them. Mara was arguing with the sisters.

Jesse changed directions, trying to lead the creatures away from her family.

"Come on," Jesse whispered. "Follow me."

She had absolutely no idea what she was doing. Nothing about this inheritance made sense, and as far as she could tell, magic sucked. Everyone kept trying to tell her stuff, and if they weren't speaking, they were bombarding her with their emotions.

Jesse stopped walking. She looked over the destroyed street scene. The creatures were angry and frustrated. She felt that much. They were acting out.

Mal had said they usually hibernated in a mine. Her magic had woken them up.

"Tell me what you need," Jesse said, raising her voice.

They chattered in response. Her hands shook, and she tried not to scream in fright.

"Angry. Frustrated." Jesse tried to feel what they felt. "Confused. Hungry?"

At that, they perked up. Pointy ears twitched.

"Are you hungry?"

Like when she'd touched the gold nugget

around her family, Jesse's vision blurred with yellow. Only this time, she saw a vision of the gremlins living in a cave. Trails of magic had come searching for a host, for Jesse. It woke the gremlins up and drove them from their home early. They searched for the food offerings meant to be there so they could hibernate for another couple of centuries, but the usual cakes and pastries weren't there. The town was gone, and they were left trying to find where the food stash was hidden.

The vision faded. Jesse slowly nodded. "Okay. I understand."

She changed her course once more for the diner. She walked carefully, but the creatures let her pass.

"Jesse." Mal shook the door, desperately trying to get to her as he fought the press of the crowd behind him.

"I'm all right, Mal," she said. "I need cake."

"What?" He frowned and leaned his ear against the glass.

"Cakes," Jesse yelled. "Pies. Giant bowls of ice cream. Candy. Every dessert you can find. And I need it to go!"

Everyone began to scramble inside the diner.

Jesse crouched next to the door to be more

on their level. "It's coming. We're sorry. We didn't know."

"The door won't open," Mal said.

"You have to have intent and focus, but not think about it."

Jesse remembered Polly's words and realized that, in her desire to escape the chaos inside, she'd also sealed the others in.

She reached to pull open the diner door. Without trying too hard, she opened it.

Mal was instantly beside her on the sidewalk. He wrapped his arms around her. Jesse felt his need to protect her and his helplessness at being unable to do so.

"They don't want to hurt us," Jesse said. "They're looking for their offerings. They think we hid them like a game."

"Here," Lily said. She and Dante appeared with pies.

Jesse took a lemon meringue and placed the tin on the ground. She slid it toward a nearby creature. The gremlin sniffed it before dipping his fingers into the creamy topping. After one taste, he instantly shoved his face into the top and began devouring it.

"Go ahead," Jesse told them.

Lily and Dante slid the other pies.

"I have cake." Mara inched forward a few

steps and set it down. Three creatures descended on it like three-year-olds needing a sugar high. They squished their clawed hands into the chocolate frosting and were soon covered.

Sal appeared with bowls of ice cream and thrust them through the cracked door. "I hope you're right about this."

Jesse pushed to her feet and took the bowls. She walked them forward and set them down.

Mal and her siblings helped pass out the food as the townsfolk handed it to them from the safety of the diner. Someone gave Mal a hamburger platter, but the gremlins only threw that back at the wall.

"Sweets," Jesse ordered. "We need sweets."

"I have sugar packets in the supply closet." Sal left only to return with three large cardboard boxes filled with sugar and sweetener packets.

"It's working." Mara pointed at the gremlin falling asleep in the lemon meringue. "Look."

Soft cheers of excitement came from the diner.

"Lily, go get the truck," Jesse said. She took the boxes from Sal to hand to Mara and Dante before keeping one for herself.

Her sister instantly went across the street. She backed up, only to drive a new path through the wrecked vehicles to get as close as possible to the diner.

Jesse dumped the sugar into the truck bed, prompting the others to do the same. The gremlins ran toward it, hopping into the truck to converge on the sugar. Jesse lifted the pie tin with the sleeping gremlin and placed it in the back.

"Make sure we got them all," Lily said through the window.

Mal gingerly carried a chocolate-covered gremlin toward the vehicle. "I think this is it."

Already more were passing out, sugar packets sticking out of their mouths.

"Mara, Dante, stay here just in case we missed some," Lily said. "And try to smooth things over with the town. Meet back at the house as soon as you can."

Mara gave Lily a pained look like she wanted to argue.

"Be careful," Dante told them.

"I'm coming too," Mal said, opening the door for Jesse. She slid into the truck and turned to watch the back as Lily reversed down the street.

"We're never going to hear the end of this from the town," Lily muttered.

"Maybe they'll be happy we saved them,"

Jesse said. "They'll see we came to their rescue and helped them."

Mal gave her a tight smile. "Yeah. Maybe."

"Nope. I bet you fifty dollars that this is going to be our fault. This is just another notch on the Crawford-Goode curse's belt." Lily switched gears and drove them toward the edge of town.

CHAPTER TEN

EPILOGUE

Two weeks later...

Jesse sat on the front porch of the bed-and-breakfast, staring at the parked vehicles in the driveway. The rental had been towed, but the deep gouges in the yard remained. Apparently, the garden gnome statues had them on their work list, but several were in recovery after trying to scare the gremlins away during the attack.

Polly had used magic to fix much of the house. The residue clung to the structure. When Jesse touched the wood frames or walked barefoot on the floor, the sensation it caused stung with intensity. Even now, the porch seemed to vibrate and hum through her clothing as she sat on the edge.

"There you are." Mal appeared from inside

the home. "They're pulling out board games if you're interested."

Jesse moved over so he could join her. "I never should have agreed to let Polly close out the apartment for me. She should have been back from Spokane by now."

Mal sat down and gave her a soft kiss before he began rubbing his hand along the small of her back in comfort. "Do you want me to fly down and check on it?"

Jesse gave a small laugh. "That's a sweet offer. What I want is to go down there myself and take care of things."

Mal smiled in understanding but didn't say anything. He didn't need to. They both knew that wasn't possible.

"It's fine," she tried to convince herself. "Polly probably just got distracted by something. A light bulb store or peanut stand or Hawaiian shirt sale."

"Herman does like a fine Hawaiian shirt," Mal agreed.

"Enough about that. How did things go today? We didn't get a chance to talk after you got back," Jesse said.

"Fine. The final paperwork has been filed. You are now a wealthy heiress," he said.

"And the nonprofit?"

"Set up. The funds will be moved over in the next month. The law firm is reviewing some of the fine points, but you should be able to start awarding grants within a few months." He smiled.

She nodded before asking in worry, "And the town?"

"Yeah, I'd give it a little more time before you venture back into town," Mal said. "They're blaming your family for sending the bad luck gremlins."

"I'm not sure I want to venture back into town," Jesse answered. Touching the gold nugget had opened her mind to receiving knowledge. Not only did she intuitively know things, but it also compelled most people to confess their deepest secrets and innermost thoughts.

Polly insisted that Jesse's new power could be used for good and that Jesse should listen and help people with their problems. That was easy to say, hard to do. Jesse did not want to hear most people's innermost secrets. One of Lily's guests had confessed to putting licked butter knives back into the drawer without washing them. His wife drank milk straight from the carton. And those were the mild confessions.

Sure, butter knives and milk cartons were questionable, but what worried Jesse was that if the wrong person confessed the wrong thing, it could put her and everyone she loved in danger. What if she came across a serial murderer, or a mob boss, or a corrupt politician who announced their sins in front of everyone?

Mal moved to take her hand in his, pulling her thoughts back to the present. "I'm not sorry you are here, but I'm sorry you're trapped here."

"It's not so bad. I like being close to Lily and Dante. I didn't realize how much I'd missed them these last few years." Jesse lifted their joined hands and pressed her cheek against the back of his. She sighed as she gazed at the view. "And it's not just my family. I have other reasons to stay."

"To learn your magic?" he asked.

"Look what I learned." Jesse lifted her free hand and wiggled her fingers. Tiny lights danced along the tips before fizzling out.

"Impressive," he agreed.

"But that was not the reason I was talking about." Jesse stood, pulling him up with her.

"Oh?"

Jesse wrapped her arms around his neck and kissed him. Love and desire swirled within her when they touched. She felt drawn to be closer to him. When she pulled away, she whispered, "Thank you for everything you've done for my family and me. I'm sorry it took me so long to get here."

"You're here now. That's all that matters." He cupped her cheek.

She felt his emotions inside of her. There were some things she didn't mind magically picking up on. "I love you, too, Malachi."

"I didn't say anything." He grinned, moving to kiss her again.

"You didn't have to. I can read every one of those thoughts in your head."

Mal kept smiling. "Oh, yeah? What am I thinking now?"

"Same thing I am." She reached into her back pocket. "I stole Cabin Four's key."

Mal reached into his pocket and pulled out his car keys. "You are a mind reader."

Jesse pulled him toward his car. "Let's get out of here before they come looking for us."

They ran to the car and climbed inside just as Lily appeared in the doorway. Jesse smiled through the window and gave a big wave at her sister as Mal quickly pulled out of the driveway so they couldn't be stopped. As they sped over the moonlit dirt road toward the cabins, Jesse felt more happiness than she'd ever experienced in her life.

"Yes, Mal, I will marry you someday." She

slid closer to him on the seat and held onto his arm as she rested her head on his shoulder.

"I didn't say anything." He moved to wrap his arm around her.

"That's all right. You didn't have to."

The End

WANT MORE OF THE LOVABLE POLLY?

Better Haunts and Garden Gnomes
Any Witch Way But Goode
A Potion for Your Thoughts

Happily Everlasting - Prequel Books
Featuring Aunt Polly
Fooled Around and Spelled in Love
Curses and Cupcakes

ABOUT MICHELLE M. PILLOW

New York Times & *USA TODAY*
Bestselling Author

Michelle loves to travel and try new things, whether it's a paranormal investigation of an old Vaudeville Theatre or climbing Mayan temples in Belize. She believes life is an adventure fueled by copious amounts of coffee.

Newly relocated to the American South, Michelle is involved in various film and documentary projects with her talented director husband. She is mom to a fantastic artist. And she's managed by a dog and cat who make sure she's meeting her deadlines.

For the most part she can be found wearing pajama pants and working in her office. There may or may not be dancing. It's all part of the creative process.

Come say hello! Michelle loves talking with readers on social media!

www.MichellePillow.com

facebook.com/AuthorMichellePillow

twitter.com/michellepillow

instagram.com/michellempillow

bookbub.com/authors/michelle-m-pillow

goodreads.com/Michelle_Pillow

amazon.com/author/michellepillow

youtube.com/michellepillow

pinterest.com/michellepillow

FEATURED TITLES FROM MICHELLE M. PILLOW

MAGICAL SCOTTISH CONTEMPORARY ROMANCES

Warlocks MacGregor®
Love Potions
Spellbound
Stirring Up Trouble
Cauldrons and Confessions
Spirits and Spells
Kisses and Curses
Magick and Mischief
A Dash of Destiny
Night Magick
A Streak of Lightning
Magickal Trouble

PARANORMAL WOMEN'S FICTION

Order of Magic Series

Second Chance Magic
Third Time's A Charm
The Fourth Power
The Fifth Sense
The Sixth Spell
The Seventh Key
The Eighth Potion

PARANORMAL SHAPESHIFTER
ROMANCES

Dragon Lords Series

Barbarian Prince
Perfect Prince
Dark Prince
Warrior Prince
His Highness The Duke
The Stubborn Lord
The Reluctant Lord
The Impatient Lord
The Dragon's Queen

To learn more about the books and to stay up to date on the latest book list visit www.MichellePillow.com

PLEASE LEAVE A REVIEW

THANK YOU FOR READING!

Please take a moment to share your thoughts by reviewing this book.

Thank you to all the wonderful readers who take the time to share your thoughts about the books you love. I can't begin to tell you how important you are when it comes to helping other readers discover the books!

Be sure to check out Michelle's other titles at https://michellepillow.com

Made in United States
Troutdale, OR
08/22/2023

12295447R00082